THE REAL DEAL:
Unscripted

Amy Kaye

SMOOCH NEW YORK CITY

For Mister Man,
a native son of my beautiful city.

SMOOCH ®

April 2004

Published by

Dorchester Publishing Co., Inc.
200 Madison Avenue
New York, NY 10016

ISBN 0-8439-5315-2

Printed in the United States of America.

Visit us on the web at www.smoochya.com.

THE REAL DEAL:

Unscripted

Prologue

I stood behind the white door, in the white hallway, with my hand on the doorknob. My other hand held the key in the lock while I waited. I could feel sweat dripping down my neck, and the microphone pack I wore on my waist was digging into my skin. I stared down at the blond wood of the floor, wondering how it got so shiny.

"Okay, go," the cameraman said.

I turned the key in the lock and opened the door.

"Hi, I'm here— Ohmigod!" I said, in what I hoped was a perfect imitation of a high school girl who's just been totally surprised.

My sister, Tina—the one I didn't know I had until a couple of weeks ago—stood in the living room, her hand on the counter of the kitchenette. She was giving me a strained smile that clearly said, "I am clinging to this counter for dear life; will you end this torture, please?"

Next to her stood Jeb Razor. I recognized him not because I know him personally, but because his face,

1

adorned with complicated facial hair and framed by a dirty-blond fringe of chin-length bangs, is currently plastered on the cover of every teen magazine in the country. He should be jetting to South Beach to party with Britney Spears, but instead he's here—in my new apartment.

And out trotted Clyde. Clyde is an adorable little bulldoggy-looking mutt who belongs to Tina and made the move to this new abode when she did. He also gets nervous around strangers. He took one look at me, the cameraman, the lights, and Jeb, and promptly squatted down and took a terrified leak, followed by a dump.

And it was all caught on film.

"Cut! Can we cut?" I asked, looking at the camera.

The cameraman shook his head.

"Can't I just come in again?" I begged. Tina was frantically scrubbing at the floor with paper towels, and Jeb was trying to soothe Clyde, who was gazing back at him, simultaneously apologetic and embarrassed (in a doggy kinda way, I guess).

The cameraman peeked his head out from behind his lens. "Strict orders," he said. "No do-overs. You know the rules."

So this would surely be the first moment of the first episode of my reality-TV show. Pardon me, can you hand me that plastic bag? I have some crap to pick up.

You know, when I first found out I was going to be on a reality-TV show, I thought it was the most exciting thing ever to hit my life. That was last year, when I was a junior at Hamilton High, in New Jersey. The biggest thrills I'd experienced were: (a) playing Fastrada in my school's production of *Pippin* and (b) being romanced and then cheated on by my then-boyfriend, Joey.

Why did I spend so much time with Joey? Correction: Why did I waste so much time on Joey? Sometimes I ponder that question. I have to admit, there was a thrill in it for me. Maybe you've done shows, and you know about the quiet anticipation of putting on makeup, doing vocal exercises, and stretching backstage when you know that just a few feet away, people are making that murmuring noise as they settle into their seats to get ready to watch you. There's a little moment of Zen silence as you stare at the curtains in the moment before they open. You feel the clutch of panic in your heart, but there's no escaping now, so you just ride it out like a wave or a dip on a roller coaster. After the show, you buzz with endorphins, feeling, for once, like everything is as it should be.

And then with Joey. He'd act so romantic, and come after me with so much intensity, and that was like a new play starting. And then I'd find out he did it again—catch him with another girl's number in his jeans pocket, or hear something, or see a girl with a hickey smirking at me like she knew some big secret—yeah, I know what your secret is. Your secret is, my boyfriend's a schmuck. The feeling then was like getting my heart ripped out of my chest, like everything had been scooped out of me.

But I kept going back. Why? I guess because feeling pain was better than feeling nothing at all. The scenes onstage, the scenes with Joey, they all blended together into one big Intense Feeling.

When the first reality show, *The Real Deal: Focus on This* started up at my high school, at first that was one more exciting event. I felt that anticipation—that curtain-going-up feeling—every morning as I put on my blush and eyeliner. The school was crawling with cameras. I could pretend I was Meryl Streep, or at least Julia Roberts, stepping over cables with professional nonchalance. And I could give them what they wanted. When I confronted Fiona, the latest of Joey's conquests, I could feel adrenaline flowing through my entire body. I shook with power. I was awesome.

Till the show aired, and I realized I was just an overwrought spaz.

Since then, I've been doing my best to keep a handle on those emotions. To that end, I got rid of the Joey monster. Buh-bye, romantic pain. So long, screaming fights. Sayonara, crying-till-I-barf.

Of course, I couldn't say good-bye to the other Intense Feeling. The performing feeling. That I'll never be able to give up. So when the network offered me my own spin-off reality show, called *Unscripted*, I said maybe. Then they told me what it entailed: I'd be cast in a Broadway play, and they'd follow my progress through rehearsals and performances. My costar would be the aforementioned Jeb, hot heartthrob du jour.

My dream come true, right?

Hang on, I'm not done.

4

My parents, the ever-pragmatic Ed and Grace Marangello, had one word to say on the subject: No. No, you can't leave high school to be on a TV show. No, you can't live in an apartment in New York City. No, the family cannot be broken apart just because your dream is coming true. No, no, *no*.

Talk about a scene. I think what went on in my house during those weeks bordered on opera.

Enter Christina. Christina Marangello. As a result of my being on *The Real Deal,* a lot of people had opinions of me. A quick perusal of various message boards, and I suddenly had a boatload of terribly creative nicknames, "bug-eyed hyper nutcase" being one of the nicer ones. People would recognize me at the mall, and they fell into two categories: those who hated the bug-eyed hyper nutcase and told me so, which sucked, because I agreed—that girl on-screen was an idiot, and she was not me. Then there were those who liked the bug-eyed hyper nutcase just as she was. Which creeped me out.

But all the attention got me one more thing: a sister.

My cell phone rang one day. I picked it up to talk to Haley, a production assistant who'd been promoted to associate producer because of a little adventure she'd helped my friends and me with. She apologized for bothering me. She admitted she should probably contact my parents first. She hemmed and hawed. Then she blurted out the secret: A woman named Tina said she was my dad's daughter from before he married my mom. A sister I'd never known about.

She'd looked into it, and it was true: his name was on the birth certificate. What did I want to do?

That was the perfect opportunity to try out my new, calm self. I cleared my throat. Said I'd call her back. Hung up the phone. Sat down. And felt myself trembling as I tried to piece it all together.

Ed Marangello is a good Catholic. He believes in family values. He keeps me on as short a leash as possible. And he's got an out-of-wedlock daughter about ten years older than me. It was shocking. Devastating. Ground-shaking. And . . . useful.

A few days later, I calmly told my parents they didn't have a leg to stand on. That I'd spoken to Tina and she wanted to have a relationship with me. That she wasn't sure if she was ready to talk to Dad. That they could try to stop us from getting to know each other if they wanted to, but they'd be hypocrites.

And then the best part: that Tina lived in New York City and had agreed to let me live with her while I was in the show. And since it taped in the summer, school wasn't an issue.

To their credit, my parents took it well. Turns out my mom knew about Tina. My dad, too, obviously. With the whole parental we-know-best, we're-perfect-role-models hypocrisy blown out of the water, they dropped their extreme bossiness and finally sat down to talk to me as an adult. My dad admitted that before he settled down, he'd had some wild years, and that Tina was the result of a little romance he'd had with a hippie girl. A girl who was nice and sweet, but who he couldn't bring home to his parents—not Italian, not Catholic, and had no desire to move to the 'burbs and produce a softball team's worth of kids. My mother shrugged. When my parents got married, they both decided it would be too confusing to acknowledge Tina and her mom as part of the family. So my dad just cut all ties with them.

I thought of my grandparents, who acted like I was the whore of Babylon for a month just because I got my ears pierced, and I could see why my parents felt that way. But I also thought of myself, and how much fun it had been to grow up in our house—the constant babble of kids, the stair-step family portraits we took every year, the amazing scent of garlic and frying onions and fra diavolo sauce that pervaded the house when my mom and aunts were making a party, and I thought, they decided that girl didn't belong here. As embarrassing as I sometimes found my grandparents' thick accents, my sisters' and brothers' loud mouths, the huge blue portrait of the Virgin Mary my mom kept in the kitchen, I knew this was a warm and wonderful place to grow up. And Tina had missed out because she was an extra, unexplainable, jagged piece of the puzzle.

"You did what you thought was best," I said, trying to be understanding and not judging of my dad. "But I don't think it was right. I want to get to know my new sister, and this is my chance to do it while I'm living out my dreams."

When I put it that way, and after a lot of talking and soul-searching, they realized I wasn't just rebelling—I was growing up. And they finally let me go.

Of course, Tina wasn't exactly thrilled with the prospect of being on camera twenty-four/seven. I

7

don't know why, it sounds like heaven to me. In the end, I guess she was so excited about getting to know me, being sisters, that she agreed before she really thought it through.

I figured she'd like it once she got used to it. She had to. Who wouldn't want to be on TV?

So that's how I ended up here, a camera on me, a sister annoyed with me, a hot guy smirking at me, and dog poop steaming up my living room.

Now, that's a party!

Chapter One

"Okay, that's plenty for tonight," the camera guy said, taking the bulky machinery away from his face. The three of us let out a collective breath of air.

"Don't get too relieved," he reminded us. "This whole apartment is miked and wired. You're on, most of the time."

"You're kidding me," Tina squeaked.

"Free apartment," I reminded her, and she nodded, swallowing hard.

"Jeb, let's go; you're supposed to be in makeup for *Letterman* already," an official-looking girl-woman-robot dressed all in black said, yanking the handsomest guy I'd ever seen out the door. He turned back to me, his green eyes flashing as he shrugged.

"Nice to meet you," he called back. "See you at rehearsal. Great dog!"

The door slammed behind him.

"Are you going to be, like, my regular guy?" I asked the cameraman.

"Yeah, most of the time," he said.

"So I can't call you Cameraman," I said.

He smiled. He was older—definitely a grown-up—but cool-looking, with mussy blond hair and a friendly attitude. "My name's Fritz," he said.

"Fritz. What's that, your first name or your last name?" I laughed.

"Just one name. Like Madonna."

"Right, I see the resemblance. Okay, see you later, Fritz." He nodded at me and Tina and left.

And then I was alone with my sister. For, like, the first time ever. I mean, we'd had some hurried meetings. Haley had arranged for us to get together, left us alone in a conference room at the network for two hours to exchange photos and try to pack in eighteen years worth of back-story, but other than that, in all the whirlwind of getting ready for the show, we hadn't been able to hang out together, just us. Standing in the kitchen, we eyeballed each other like kids at the bus stop on the first day of kindergarten.

"So, um," I said.

"Yeah. This is weird." She laughed.

"Oh! Let me help with that." I grabbed a paper towel myself, and some cleaning spray from under the sink. Everything was brand-new and antiseptic. After my rambling, comfortably messy home, where the color brown was the default choice (easier to clean, doesn't show dirt), this white-walled, blond-floored apartment made me feel like I was living in a hospital.

Tina and I knelt down together, making sure the little accident was cleaned up, as Clyde gazed at us with a look of extreme worry and guilt. We finally sat back, finished. The polished wood floor was as pale and shiny as ever.

I crossed my legs, and Tina kind of pulled hers under her. Her flowing, flowery dress covered everything but her tiny pale feet. I felt like a big Pokémon next to a fragile porcelain doll.

"We don't really look alike," I said.

"No?" she asked. We turned and looked in the floor-to-ceiling mirrors along the living room wall. "Well, you're dark," she said. "Like our dad in those pictures you showed me. And from what I remember, when I was small and he used to come see us sometimes. But we both have brown eyes."

"Yours look so striking," I said. "They're surprising. Because you're so fair, otherwise."

"My mom's even paler," she said. "You can practically see right through her."

I thought of my own mom, a little olive-skinned fireplug with comfy breasts and hips that could hold a hundred babies. "Uh-huh," I said.

"We've got the same eyes," she pointed out. "Just in a different frame."

I tried to see it, but it was tough. There I was: crazy curly brown hair bursting out from my head, tanned olive skin, and curves everywhere, no matter how many meals I skipped. My legs were pure muscle from all my years of dancing. Even my hands looked large and peasantlike, as if I were supposed to be smashing grapes or olives or something. And Tina seemed made for the shade, for a stately manor and the cool cave of a carriage drawn by horses. Well, maybe I was

11

reading too much into the situation. We were sisters, anyway.

"So did you take today off from work?" I asked.

Tina nodded. "I haven't had a day off in, like . . . oh, God, since I started at this law firm," she said. "I've been working around the clock. I keep a suit at the office in case I have to pull an all-nighter, you know?"

I nodded, though I had no idea.

"I'm really glad we're here," she said. "I'm glad we're together."

"Well, I'm sorry if it's more of a shock than you expected," I told her. "You're not that comfortable with being filmed all the time, are you?"

"Nooo . . ." she admitted. "Actually, I kind of hate it. But my student loans are killing me, and the free apartment for the summer helps a lot. But . . . oh. I really don't like being in the spotlight. It was bad enough when I was a kid."

"What do you mean? You were on TV?"

"No. But my mom . . . she's a character. She really stands out; she's always doing something strange. When I was small, she'd pick me up from school wearing these bright, fancy hippie clothes that just mortified me. She was a yoga instructor, and always had a different boyfriend. In grade school, everyone thought she was weird. In high school, everyone thought she was cool, and expected me to be like her. I just . . ." Tina shook her head. "I just wanted to be normal."

"God, that's the last thing I ever wanted to be." I snorted.

12

"Because you had it," she said. "You had a mom . . . and you had Dad."

God. I'm such an idiot. Of course—I had her dad. And she didn't.

"I'm sorry," I said.

"No. No, it's not your fault," she said, looking sad.

"So you used to know him before—"

"Before he settled down. Yeah." Tina nodded. "I think I only saw him four times or so. I mean I'm sure he saw me when I was a baby, but then, when I was walking around—it's sort of murky, you know, memories from when you're so young feel like dreams. I remember being small and feeling this unfamiliar hand holding mine, and looking up and seeing this dark being. He wasn't scary. I loved his smell, the way he'd throw me in the air. He'd take me down to the playground by the river, and it was exciting to be out without my mom. But when we got back, it was a relief, too."

"And then he just stopped coming?"

Tina fondled Clyde's soft, triangle-shaped ears as he lolled around in her lap, patting her with a pale, black-nailed paw. "Yeah. I'd ask my mom every once in a while. 'Remember that Daddy man? Where did he go?' Like he was an imaginary friend or a pet that ran away. And she'd just hug me and say, 'He'd like to be here, but he can't, so it's just you and me, chickadee.'"

She paused. "'Just you and me, chickadee.' Whenever she said that, I felt like we had the whole world, everything we needed. But I missed his big hands, that smell, the feeling of being thrown up in

13

the air. I missed it so much it hurt, like the hole left when a tooth falls out. So I packed it away and tried to forget about it. I moved on. I stopped asking. I couldn't change it, so I ignored it."

Clyde made a snuffling sneeze and I looked down at my own lap, wishing I had something to fidget with. I felt ashamed, lucky, angry, sad.

"I mean, it wasn't always so great," I said, remembering how my parents would shout and argue as one of my younger brothers or sisters wailed in a bassinet. How I knew more about changing diapers and doing laundry and administering time-outs than an eighteen-year-old has a right to. How easy it was to get lost in the babble, become one of a crowd, in my own home. How I could crave just a moment alone, and feared it, too.

"Of course. I know," Tina said, looking at me and nodding with an expression that made me feel like she could see the thoughts in my head. "I just missed him sometimes. It would have been nice to know he thought about me, that he was proud of the things I learned to do. It turned into a little ice-cube in my heart. It was terrible to not know who he was, and to grow up not knowing. But it would be more terrible not to take advantage of this. Of finding you."

She looked up at the cameras in the corners of the room and gave a little grimace of a smile. "Hey, I can deal with being on TV. If it's important to you, I can do it. Anyway, the producers promised I wouldn't be on screen that much. The show's about you, not about your home-life drama."

I didn't tell her what I'd found out about producers and their promises. The night was going too well.

"There's no food in that brand-new fridge," I informed her. "And it's so clean, I don't even want to put anything in it."

She laughed. "Well, don't worry about it—we're half a block from Carmine's. The best Italian food you can get outside of Little Italy. I'd love to hear how it compares to what you grew up eating. Come on, I'll buy us some macaroni."

Tina and I caught up over identical plates of rigatoni alla buttera.

"So you were in the city this whole time?" I asked. "So close?"

"No, sometimes we lived up in Woodstock," she told me. "We moved around a lot. For a couple of years we lived in Virginia. I liked that. My mom's boyfriend was this big guy named Rufus, and he was really nice to us. I guess they had a falling-out when she . . . Well, I don't know what happened." She shook her head. "My mom's a wonderful person, but she's a handful." She looked up at me. "What about you? You were so close to the city, you guys must have come here a lot."

"Not really. I mean, it was a big outing, all of us piling in the station wagon to see a Broadway show once a year at Christmastime. We'd go to the Jersey shore for a couple weeks in the summer. Um . . . and school trips, I guess. I remember they brought us in to see a big Degas show. That was cool. But, you know, it's not like I came in by myself. My parents were terrified I'd get kidnapped by a white-slave ring, or something."

"Christmasses," Tina said, and smiled.

"What? You guys did Christmas, right? I mean, I know you're not Catholic, but—"

"Not really. I got winter solstice presents. And a Barbie doll was out of the question. I'd get, like, a Native American dream catcher."

"Oh, jeez," I said. "Well, you know. Maybe by Christmastime you'll want to . . . come see what our Christmas is like."

Tina winced. "I don't know if I'm ready," she said. "I've been so mad at your dad—I mean, our dad— for so long. For dumping us. I always suspected he had ditched us for a nice, normal family with a nice, quiet wife, and it turns out—"

"Well, my mom's not quiet," I said. "She's a yeller."

"Huh. So . . . yeah, I guess it's not exactly what I thought."

"It's funny, though," I said.

"What?"

"I mean, looking at you. You seem so normal. Kind of straitlaced, even. I mean you'd never suspect—"

"Hey!" We were interrupted by a friendly-looking guy in painter's pants, a bowling shirt, and Vans, holding a skateboard. "I thought I'd find you here."

"Jonah!" Tina blinked up at him. "What—"

"I know, I know you said you wanted to be alone with your sister, but I had to come by," he said. "It's too crazy. You're kidding!" He looked at me, with a grin so wide I had no choice but to return it. "You're

16

Tina's sister? You look about as alike as two peas in completely different pods."

I busted out laughing, and Tina moved over so he could sit down. Despite her surprise, I saw her get softer and smilier now that he was here.

"So are you Tina's boyfriend?" I asked.

Jonah grinned even wider. "I say I am; she says I'm a pain in the butt."

"Oh, come on, let's not—" Tina objected.

"Okay, we won't," he said, playfully tugging at her shoulder. "Seriously, we just hang out. When she'll let me. And she's not working. Which is about once a year, I guess. Hey, are you eating that?"

I gratefully handed him my fork, as there was enough on my plate to feed a medium-size army.

"How did you guys meet?" I asked, glad to have something to talk about besides the fact that Tina was totally resentful of my perfect, boring life. "Don't tell me. She was your lawyer when you got run over by a truck and had to sue the driver?"

"Not Tina! She's a corporate lawyer, don'tcha know," Jonah snickered. "Hides in her office and writes contracts while the partners do all the arguing in court."

"What? That's crazy!" I shot Tina a look.

She shrugged. "I like paper," she said.

"No, she came wheeling into the store where I work," Jonah said. "It's a skateboard store, and she needed some new wheels on her rollerblades."

"It's the only exercise I get," she interjected.

"You've got to see this girl on the blades," Jonah told me. "She's a machine."

"Little Tina? I thought she'd break."

"Oh, no. Don't let her birdlike stature fool you. Tina blades like she works—like she's always under a deadline."

"Well, there's no reason to dawdle."

"She came in, and I talked her into getting some Kryptonic wheels with skulls on them. And I upgraded her to a better helmet, the better to protect her own pretty little cranium."

"Oh, brother." Tina rolled her eyes.

"By the time she was done, I was smitten, and she hasn't been able to shake me since."

"He keeps saying he wants to show me tricks, but I can't see the point," Tina told me.

I was starting to be a little smitten myself. Not like I had the hots for Jonah—he was clearly head over heels for Tina, and was a little too crunchy for my tastes—but he was just so likable, it was amazing. I loved the funny way he talked. "Her birdlike stature"? Who talks like that? He said everything like it was a funny punch line he'd just thought up, which I guess it was.

I caught Tina stealing some affectionate glances in his direction. So even though it was mostly him pouring on the charm, she liked him too, I decided. She just wasn't as obvious about it as some other people I could mention. Like me. Or like I used to be, with Joey.

Ugh. *Forget about Joey. This isn't about boys; this is about furthering my professional development,* I told myself.

"Well, kids, I'm going to head home," I said, standing and excusing myself. "What's my half, like, ten bucks?"

"Forget it, my treat," Tina said. "I'll meet you soon. We've both got to be up early tomorrow," she said, more to Jonah than to me, as if to warn him not to even try to get her to stay out.

"Just one cocktail," he said. "And a walk to that little park?"

"One walk," she told him sternly. I shook my head, laughing, and excused myself.

It wasn't that long before I heard Tina come in. I'd taken a shower, in a bathroom as white as the rest of this spanking-new place, and was lying in bed, staring out the window, patting Clyde with soothing strokes as if it were him, not me, who was nervous about starting rehearsals in the morning.

Tina knocked. "Come in," I said, and I saw the door open a crack in the dim light. She'd put on her jammies and looked even more like a little girl.

"So?" she said.

"Come on in here," I told her.

She ran over and hopped into my bed and we lay there, listening to the hum of the air conditioner, watching the orange sky refusing to get any darker than raw umber.

"I always thought this was what I'd do if I had a sister," she said.

"We do this at home all the time," I told her. "Mom never knows where to find us. We play musical bedrooms, depending on who's mad at who."

"Wow. There are seven of you, right?" She tugged

19

on Clyde's ear and he blinked at her with the same adoring gaze that Jonah had given her.

I grinned. "Lucky seven. I'm the oldest. Or I was, before you came along."

"Yowza." She grinned back at me.

"So what's with this guy?" I asked her. "You didn't even mention him."

"Oh, I can't get serious about Jonah," she scoffed. "He's a skate kid."

"He's your age!" I pointed out. "Twenty-seven. He's not a kid."

"He's a kid in . . . Oh, he's just a kid," she said. "He doesn't even have health insurance. He works as a retail salesperson and does skateboard competitions. I'm a lawyer. It wouldn't work."

I listened to the gentle sound of the traffic far below and didn't say anything. It was a new thing I was trying: not opening my mouth. I thought it was a shame to waste the kind of love that Jonah obviously had for Tina. But it wasn't my business. I had to get to know my sister, and I had to get ready to start rehearsals. The last thing I wanted to do was lecture her with my know-it-all attitude and get into an argument. Musical bedrooms doesn't work so well when it's just the two of you, you know?

"Whatever you think," I said.

"Well, I'll probably be gone by the time you get up," Tina said. "So good luck tomorrow, okay? I'll fix the coffeemaker so all you have to do is turn it on when you get up. Double-check your alarm, please."

I did. It was set.

"You'll be great tomorrow," she said, smoothing my sproingy hair as she got up.

I grabbed her hand. "Tina, thanks," I said.

"For what?"

"For doing this. I know it goes against your grain."

"Well, thanks to you," she told me.

"For what?"

"For showing up. Sister."

She boinked my nose with her finger and tousled Clyde's ears. "Don't let him take up the whole bed," she told me. And she padded out of the room.

I lay there alone, not really believing this was my life. It was exciting. Awesome. I felt like Belle and Ariel and Cinderella all rolled into one. With an urban soundtrack and a sweet, smelly dog. I guess I finally fell asleep. The last thing I remember was the faraway beeping of a car and the red neon light across the street clunking into darkness.

Chapter Two

"How do I look?" I asked Fritz. He didn't answer, so I peered into the darkness of his lens to make sure there wasn't any lipstick on my teeth. It involved baring my teeth like a demented terrier.

"You won't let them put that in the show, will you?" I giggled. He finally gave in.

"You know I'm not supposed to talk to you," he said from behind his lens.

"I know, but I'm nervous," I complained. "My tummy's been acting up all morning."

"No details, please," he said. "You look fine. You'd better get in there."

I sighed and pulled down my T-shirt. I'd chosen my rehearsal clothes with the kind of intensity that, like, I didn't even give to my junior prom outfit. My good-luck black tights, which I wore for my audition at the New Jersey Arts Festival, are ripped, which makes me love them more. A plain leotard with a safety pin pulling the front of the scoop neck into a V-neck. The aforementioned T-shirt, which was so tattered it basically hung off me. I mean, I wanted to look like I had just pulled everything off the floor and put it on, but that my fashion sense was so inborn that I couldn't help but look good.

Come on, give me a break. I said I was nervous, right?

A word, before I step into rehearsal, about this play I'm in. A couple of years ago, a young writer and his male lover wrote a different kind of musical—one that dispensed with tap-dancing chorus girls, shiny costumes, and most of all, a happy ending.

Don't get me wrong: I've got nothing against tap-dancing chorus girls in shiny costumes. I hope to be one before too long. But this show, *Twentynothings* is unbelievable. The music sounds more like rock than Broadway, and the songs are about real stuff—people trying to find their way in the world, doing the wrong thing, and sometimes failing. Love that goes stupidly wrong. Young adults who grew up in their various ways—some with advantages, some not so much—and get themselves into trouble. And have to dig their way out. And want to sing their hearts out in the process.

The story's like this: This guy, Daniel seems to have it all. He's a stockbroker and living in Chelsea with his best friend from home, Steve. Steve's got no money, because he's in grad school, so he's sort of beholden to Daniel, but they're best friends, you know, so it should be okay. Except Daniel has a dark secret: He's totally addicted to drugs, and it's starting to make his world fall apart.

This is where the play gets kind of R-rated. Daniel

has this kind of on-again, off-again girlfriend, Tinka. She's the total opposite of him, a Lower East Side, squatter-type, and she's just in it for the nookie, if you know what I mean. He doesn't have time for a steady girl, so he booty-calls her in this dysfunctional just-for-sex relationship. Only she sees what's happening to him, and she can't help but get emotionally involved, despite the fact that she swears she has no emotions.

Meanwhile, the roommate, Steve, sees that his friend is in trouble, but he's got problems of his own. His fiancée, Dannica, is perfect in every way, and they have a whole life planned together, only he's got his own secret—he's really gay, and he doesn't know how to bust out of his role and live the life he wants. He starts to fall in love with a wild, beautiful drag queen who lives downstairs, yet fights it with every fiber of his being—and Dannica slowly starts to realize her perfect future is just not going to happen.

It's totally heartbreaking. The relationship with Tinka and Daniel is just so intense: They realize they are in love, and that's so amazing, and then the drugs are too much to contend with, and they break up—Daniel turns on Tinka viciously when she tries to get him to kick the habit. I'm telling you, you've never seen such an intense experience portrayed on a stage.

The first time I saw it—I mean, I've seen the show like three times—I knew I had to be in it. And I also knew every row of that theater had a girl in it like me, swearing on a stack of leg warmers that she was going to grace that stage someday. So being in this show—playing Tinka as Jeb played Daniel wasn't just about the thrill of being on Broadway. It was about being in the exact Broadway show I'd loved since I was eight. It was realizing a dream on top of a dream. So excuse me if I was worried about lipstick and tights on the first day of rehearsal. This, my friend, was majorly major.

So. Deep breath. I pushed open the door of the theater and walked into the gloom. At the other end of the aisle was the stage, with no-fanfare worklights making it look just as ordinary as the stage in Hamilton High. The one where I'd gotten multiple standing ovies for my portrayal of Fastrada when I was just a freshman. The stage is my friend. I walked forward, willing my knees to stop shaking.

I tried to size up the other girls, but they were larger-than-life. A beautiful black girl with hair down to her butt was in a split, stage right (that's the actor's right, for you audience members), and was arching first to the right, then to the left, to stretch her hamstrings. Center stage was this little redheaded girl, just tiny, but with the kind of curvy, strong body that makes guys stop talking in midsentence every time they even think about it. She was running through some dance steps, and it was clear: Not only did she have the intricate choreography down cold, but she also added charisma and spirit to every step. No wonder she was here.

Oh, and I was here too.

Why was that again?

I wanted to turn and run out of there, but frankly, my legs would have collapsed under me. So I kept walking until I reached the stage and put my rehearsal bag down, making just enough of a clunk so the director, Seth Morrison, noticed I was there.

"Hey," he said, turning to greet me. "And hey," he said to Fritz, who gave him a wave from his behind-the-camera stance.

"Howdy," I said. "So I'm here." Duh. Obviously. Shut up, Claire.

"Right. So do whatever warm-up you usually do and we'll get started."

Whatever warm-up I usually do? I don't know! Mrs. Wilson, the faded Broadway starlet who directs all of Hamilton's shows, usually puts us through a whole rigorous hour-long class before we start rehearsal. I hopped onto the stage, stepping over the athletic, preppy-looking guy who played Steve, and walked past the few other cast members in a way I hoped would appear nonchalant.

"That's mine," the redhead said when I reached for the metal folding chair near her. "You can get one backstage."

I did, and when I came back to the stage, picking a spot that seemed out of the way, the African-American girl came over to sit on it while I used it as a barre for my warm-up. I tried to hear Mrs. Wilson's commanding voice in my head as I struggled to remember what she'd made us do.

"Don't mind Paula," the black girl said to me in a deep, throaty British accent. "She's trying to be alpha dog, and I just let her think she's succeeding. She idolized the girl who had your part before you came, so I guess she thinks it's her turn to be the star."

"Evelyn Boquart? I saw her—she was amazing," I said. "I don't blame her for idolizing her."

"Well, you'll be good, too," she told me.

I smiled. "Hope so," I said. "Where is your accent from? Are you English?"

"African," she said. "From Tanzania. I walk into auditions and everyone assumes I'm going to sound like Missy Elliott. Boy, does it shock them when I open my mouth and out comes BBC News Radio."

"I think it's cool," I said. I looked around. "Wait a minute. There's someone missing from the cast. Don't tell me you're—"

"Playing Kelvin the drag queen? Indeed I am," she laughed. "It's a bit of nontraditional casting, but I've got the seal of approval from the fellows at Lucky Cheng's, so I must be doing something right."

"Lucky Cheng's?"

"A restaurant in the East Village that has an all-drag staff. They let me work there as I studied for the role. They think it's a riot, though I think they're also a bit jealous."

"Wow." I looked her up and down. "A girl playing a guy playing a girl. That's very *Victor/Victoria*."

"It's very Malaika."

"Malaika?"

"That's my name. It means 'Angel.' But in my family, it also means 'marches to the beat of her own damn drummer.' "

"I think that's what Claire must mean, too," I said, and we both laughed. She brushed her long dread-locks out of her face and pulled them up into a po-nytail. "Good luck."

"Hey," I said, before she could desert me to stretch all alone.

"Yeah?" She arched an eyebrow at me.

"Seth. Is he cool?"

"He's hard to read," she admitted. "I can never tell if he's happy with my performance. I know when he's pissed, but it's all I can do to figure out if I've done a good job."

"Great." I sighed. "That's what I thought from the meeting I had with him, but I wasn't sure."

"Just try to forget about the cameras and do your best," she told me. "We need it."

"I know. It's tough to have us non-professionals forced on you—"

"Not that." Malaika shook her head. "People get cast for all sorts of reasons, and it always seems to come out all right in the end if you just work together. I'm talking about the whole show. We're in trouble."

"You mean, like money trouble?" I resumed my stretches, turning my back to the others so we had a little private workout area of our own. Malaika bent herself in half, doing her own amazing stretches, and nodded as she did it.

"The production company took you on as a last-ditch effort to get the show back on its feet," she said. "You came along at just the right time—losing those other actors to their Hollywood projects was a real blow. We have to do well with this cast—they don't even have money to pay understudies."

"Ohmigod," I said. "What if I break my leg?"

She fixed me with a stare. "Don't," she advised.

She winked and stretched again.

29

So I had a little more pressure than I thought. But it looked like I also had a friend. Not bad for the first ten minutes of my first rehearsal of my first Broadway show.

The doors of the theater opened again, but this time there was no missing who was walking in. It was Jeb, and he was surrounded by handlers chattering at him like a crowd of paparazzi. He walked with his head down, hands in his pockets, like he was trying to be low-key, but there was just no way. That same public-relations girl was jabbering at him, talking about schedules and appearances, and some kind of wardrobe person was on the other side, talking on her cell phone about the costume and how it would have to be altered to flatter him more. I could see even the unflappable Fritz was distracted—his camera swung around to take in the spectacle.

Finally, Jeb reached the lip of the stage and turned around.

"Guys, I have to get to work," he said.

They kept talking. Jeb grabbed one of them, a bald guy, and whispered in his ear. It looked like he was absolutely begging this guy to get this crowd of hangers-on to take a hike.

"Come on, people," the bald guy called out. "Let's let the star get on with his rehearsal."

"But what about his appearances?" the PR girl piped up.

The bald guy looked back at Jeb, beseechingly, but Jeb just shook his head.

"Not now," the bald guy insisted, and herded the disappointed posse-members out of the theater. The whole group plodded out, so full of dejection that an actual rain cloud over their heads wouldn't have been a surprise. Jeb shook his head, then stood up straighter, as if the group of handlers had been an actual weight that was gone now. He turned around and looked up at our director.

"Sorry," he said to Seth, who gave a tight smile and shook his head. Seth was tall, had a shaved head (as opposed to just being bald—there's a difference, mostly in terms of sexiness), and wore a perpetual expression of annoyance. Right now his annoyance seemed earned. I felt for him, actually. The producers of this play he was directing had saddled him with not one, but two stars who weren't real Broadway actors. Sure, we might bring in some new audiences, which was really important with the economy being in so much trouble—theater was really suffering. But that didn't make us any easier to work with. I promised myself I'd do my best for him.

"Come on," Seth said, waving Jeb onto the stage. "Everyone's warming up, then we're going to do a readthrough and some vocal work."

The thing is, even with his posse banished from the room, Jeb had some kind of magnetic quality. We all kept stealing glances at him. It wasn't just that he was good-looking. There were other cute guys in the cast and crew. It was like he was shiny from somewhere deep inside. The denim of his jeans looked softer and cleaner. His hair had something in it that made it lie differently from everyday hair. Everything about him seemed utterly different from the rest of us, like we were mutts and he was a purebred Doberman pinscher. I guess that's what celebrity does. Or maybe it's what makes you a celebrity. Either way, he had it, and it was a little distracting.

But in a nice way.

Three hours later, I was wishing Jeb were ten times more distracting. At least to Seth. That promise I had made, to make his job easier by being the best Tinka (that's the name of my character) I could be? Yeah, that wasn't good enough. Apparently the best Tinka I could be was the worst Tinka he'd ever seen.

"Stop!" he roared. "What the hell was that? Try it from the top again."

Our read-through finished, and a few songs gone over, we'd decided to try blocking a big musical number. Never mind that we were onstage, not in a studio, so there was no mirror for me to check my form in while I worked. Never mind that this was the first time I was trying this choreography. Never mind that this was my first day, and we'd already been going at it for hours. Seth was pissed, and I was screwing up even worse because of it.

"I wish we could just get through this once," Paula muttered to herself (loudly).

"It wasn't all that long ago you were tripping over your own damn feet," Malaika said, full voice, giving Paula a killer glare.

"Who's talking to you?" Paula sniffed. But she moved slightly farther from Malaika, as if she were worried that a particularly high kick could accidentally hit her right in the keister.

It should have made me feel better, but I was too

32

mortified from not getting the choreography right. Paula was being mean, but she was also one hundred percent correct. I was a mess, and I was slowing everyone else down. I had two weeks to get in shape for my debut in the show, and unless a week was going to magically stretch to about six months, the show was in deep doo-doo.

"Settle down, Girl Scouts," Seth warned us. "Let's take it again, please, from the top. A-five-six-seven-eight . . ."

We put ourselves through our paces again, crossing and recrossing the stage in different versions of twentysomething New Yorkers running to and from their sometimes-fabulous, sometimes-boring jobs. This number was supposed to set the scene and let the audience see that the city was a wild mix of every kind of person in the world, but I seemed to be a plodding, draggy black hole right in the middle of it—like a tacky tourist in the middle of a Chanel runway show.

"And turn, and kick—layout, Claire, good!" Malaika muttered as I took one of my turns across the stage. When we danced together, she kept up her encouraging monologue, chanting the steps so that I could at least keep up, if not in the style I would have liked. She even managed to stay half a step ahead of what we were really doing—I mean, can you imagine being so coordinated that you can call out one step while you're doing a whole other one? The girl was spectacular. And I was so grateful. I felt like I was being buoyed up by her help, like her words

33

were doing the dancing for me, and I began to relax a little and even, maybe, halfway enjoy myself.

Until I saw Jeb do his thing. He had a solo right in the middle of the number. Now, here's one thing I know about Jeb: He started rehearsal the exact same day I did. So how come he had not only picked up the whole solo—but he was also, like, a perfect complement to the other dancers onstage?

I knew why. Because he had talent, and I was sucky.

Filled with the lead of this new realization, I started what was supposed to be my solo. I was too far away from Malaika to hear anything she had to say, and anyway, nobody was whispering in Jeb's ears. And he seemed to manage just fine. I was the only one onstage too idiotic to pick this up, and there was no reason to—

"Oh, please, you're killing me. . . . *Stop!*" Seth bellowed.

I stopped.

"For God's sake, it's a simple matter of getting yourself across the stage with a modicum of grace, Claire. You look like you're marching into the dentist's office for a root canal. This is supposed to be fun. Light. Airy and energetic. It's not performance art, or whatever else you were doing up there!"

Did you ever have that dream where you're in school and suddenly you realize you're naked? That's how I felt. Exposed, humiliated, and utterly point-and-laughable. It was total and utter embarrassment. There was no way it could get worse, unless . . .

Ugh. I felt it. First the trembling in my chin, then a

34

horrible, moist, brimming feeling in my eyes. A tickle in my tear ducts. Sweat on my palms. And a clutch in my heart.

"Oh, you're not going to *cry!* Don't you have any control at all? What the hell is this, cheerleader try-outs? Can someone help me? I thought I was directing a goddamn Broadway show here!" Seth ranted.

And then it happened. That old panicked feeling, the one I had held at bay for months and months, since my breakup with Joey and my freakout at Fiona in the atrium of our high school. Everything went white, and I burst out crying. The world felt like it was absolutely, totally ending—there was no reason to live, no reason to keep trying, and certainly no reason to stop crying.

I was, I'll admit, in total over-the-top drama queen mode.

"I don' know what you wan' from meeeee," I screeched. "I cannot *do this* when you *yell at me!* Jus' stop *yelling* and maybe I could *do it,* you *ass-hole!*"

"Very nice," Seth said, turning to the imaginary audience. "The girl from reality TV is calling me an asshole. I hope they have a good bleeper on this show."

"I don' care whad they haaave," I wailed. "I don' care, 'cuz i quit!" Deep gasp of air that sounds like a dying whale. "Ya hear me? I *quiiiiiit!*"

With that, I leaped down from the stage and ran out of the theater as if I were being chased by Tony Soprano. I didn't know where to go—workers were milling about in the lobby, I guess painting it or something—so I ran into the bathroom and let out a giant sob that felt like it was going to split my chest in two.

I cried in huge, heaving, completely inelegant gasps. I'm telling you, when I lose my temper, there is no finding it—and it had been a while, so this was a doozy. I was in the midst of a total hissy fit, and it took about two minutes of wheezing, dry-heaving, and boogering up the joint before I realized what a totally stupid, self-indulgent, idiotic, horrible move I had just made.

I hated myself.

I replayed the scene in my head and realized I should not have flipped out at all. I'd tripped over my own two feet—first literally, then figuratively, when I overreacted to Seth's abusive rant. Okay, so I wanted to cry. Did I have to yell?

Apparently I did. And now that I was calm, I realized that my rehearsal bag (which contained my keys, my wallet, and my cell phone) was sitting dejectedly in the first row of seats, next to the stage.

And I was here.

I splashed freezing-cold water on my face and tried to figure out what to do. I could hear Fritz padding back and forth outside the bathroom door. He'd obviously caught my whole "performance" on tape and was waiting to see what happened next. Well, I didn't feel like giving it to him.

Looking up, I saw the kind of thing you only see in movies: one of those little half windows, way up high above the stalls. Hmm. I couldn't leave through the door. And I couldn't stay in that bathroom forever. So I did the only thing I could do: Still dressed in my rehearsal rags, I climbed up to the top of the stalls, then shimmied carefully out that dirty little window.

It must have looked like the big brick theater was giving birth, or leaking high school–aged girls, or something. But the only person who noticed me was a mild-looking, ancient Chinese man (well, I suppose I should call him Asian—but I'm pretty sure he was Chinese). He looked up at me, halfway out the window, and raised his eyebrows.

"Could you possibly . . .?" I asked.

He raised his hands over his head, and I grabbed them. The old dude was surprisingly strong. I used him as, like, leverage so I could wiggle my hips out and, in a typically ungraceful move, yank my legs out of the window and land with a *clop* on the ground.

"What you doing up there?" he asked, amazed.

"I had to . . . um, leave," I said, totally lamely.

"You need to use the door next time."

"Good idea," I told him, again sounding like a total idiot. He shook his head in amusement (and maybe a little disgust) and kept walking down the street.

So there I was. No keys, no money, nothing—except my freedom. And I was standing on Forty-second Street dressed like a demented hooker. Now, this was showbiz.

Chapter Three

It took about zero seconds for me to realize that no matter how clean and Disneyfied Midtown got, it was no place for a barely-eighteen-year-old who's half-dressed and still has puffy, red eyes. (Very few places are, if you think about it.) Without stopping to consider my options, I practically sprinted back to my apartment building, a block away, and elicited only one or two wolf whistles.

Once I was safely inside the glass doors of my cool, marble-floored lobby, I leaned my back against the wooden panels that lined it and smiled ingratiatingly at Carlton, my doorman.

"Hey, Carlton," I said, as if running around in a leotard were par for the course for a sassy starlet like me.

"Rough day?" he asked, eyeing the new rip in my tights.

"Ah . . . yeah," I said. I cleared my throat. "Do you have ayyyyyyy—sparekeyformyapartment?" I asked in a rush, terrified that he'd say no and I'd have to burst into tears again.

He reached beneath the desk and pulled out something shiny, jangly, and remarkably keylike.

"You can't disappear with this," he said. "I only have one extra."

"I won't!" I promised him. "I will not disappear with it for even one minute. I swear, I'll bring it right back down as soon as I—"

Hm. As soon as I what? It dawned on me that I had no idea what to do next.

"Just make sure you bring it back," Carlton said with a weary shake of his head. I guess he'd seen it all. Or I was just too weird for him to be around. Either way, I didn't care. I grabbed the keys, shouted a thank-you over my shoulder, and sprinted for the elevators.

Once upstairs and safely inside my apartment, I collapsed on a bar stool in the kitchenette. It's hard to collapse on a bar stool—it takes a certain amount of balance and coordination—but that's exactly what I did. My head clunked down on the counter, and I clunked it a few more times for good measure.

"Stupid, stupid, stupid," I scolded myself. "Stupid, immature, stupid, asshole, stupid." With that, I remembered myself calling Seth, my director, an asshole, and I clunked my head harder.

"Stupid!" I moaned. Then I realized, with a shock, that I was on camera—without Fritz being anywhere near me. I looked up and sure enough, the little glass eye in the upper corner of the kitchen had focused

its little round self squarely on me. I couldn't even chill out without being spied on.

I clunked my head down for the last time and just stayed there. "Stuuuupid," I moaned, giving up utterly.

That was all there was time to do before the phone started ringing. I glared up at the white receiver, trilling like an old-time opera singer, and said, "Shut up."

It did not comply. I picked it up.

"Claire?" I heard someone say sharply. It was Haley, from the production company of *Unscripted*.

"Yah," I moaned.

"What the hell is going on?" she shouted. "You quit? What happened? I got a call from Seth and he's ready to—"

"Can you hold on? I've got another call," I said. With her voice still making a staccato, tinny rhythm in the earpiece, I hit flash and said, "Hello?"

"Are you okay? It's Malaika!"

"If you call being a stupid moron okay, then I'm great," I said.

"Just hang in there. Worse things have happened. Divas have tantrums all the time."

"Divas earn their tantrums," I told her.

"So you're getting a head start."

"I've got to go," I told her, and clicked back to Haley.

". . . took a chance on you, and you can't just disappear! I can't have this kind of—"

"Sorry, another call again," I said, and hit flash once more.

41

"Claire? Claire, is that you?"

"Tina? Yeah, it's me."

"Are you all right? Are you hurt?"

"Of course. I mean, no! I'm not hurt." Why did she sound so scared?

"The production office called me. They had me paged at my office when they couldn't find you. They said you disappeared. Ran away. Did you run away?"

Uuuuuggh. Now I clunked my head against the column that held the phone. "No, no, I didn't run away—I am so sorry they bothered you at work," I said.

"It's okay," Tina said. "I mean, not really, but I'm glad you're okay." I heard her murmur to someone in her office. "I'm sorry," she said. "I'll be right there. Just one more moment. I'm sorry!"

"You go, Tina, go ahead," I said, even more mortified than I'd been onstage a half hour earlier. "I'm fine. I'm sorry. I didn't mean for you to be . . . interfered with, or whatever."

"Okay. I do have to go. Then nothing's wrong?"

"No. No, it was a misunderstanding."

Now she sounded pissed. "Well, Claire, really, if it's not an emergency, just please handle it, okay? I'm kind of under the gun over here."

"Sorry. Sorry," I said again, and she clicked off.

Way to go, Claire.

The phone rang the second I hung it up and I realized Haley was still on hold. I picked it up, expecting to hear her yelling.

"I'm sorry," I said immediately.

"Claire? Is that you? It's Fiona! You didn't pick up

your cell, so I called home on the off chance—hold on, why did you say you're sorry?"

I guess Haley had gotten tired of waiting and hung up. My body flooded with relief to hear my friend on the other end, her voice jumping through the wire like a happy puppy. "Oh, my God, Fiona, I screwed up so bad," I moaned.

"What? What happened?"

I told her everything. The crappy dance moves I'd tried to bust, the humiliation of getting everything wrong, and the triple humiliation of throwing a fit about it. Fiona knew all about my hissy tantrums. She'd seen enough of them. But I described this one in wince-worthy detail, as if I were punishing myself for my utter lack of control.

In the background, as I talked, I could hear a crackly announcement over the PA system at the Hamilton public pool, where Fiona was working as a lifeguard with Baxter for the summer. I felt the biggest pang just then, and felt like I was wrapped in a thick, hot blanket of homesickness. It lurched through me. I stopped talking just to listen to every summer of my life up till then.

"Oh, Claire, you've been through this before," Fiona reminded me. "You had an on-camera upset, and you survived. But that's not even the important thing. The show is the show—you'll look good or bad depending on how they edit you; you can't worry about that. What matters is that you get to be on Broadway because of that dumb TV show, and you have to go back and try again."

"Try again! Sure! Right after I stick a hot poker in my eye!" I yelped.

"You are an amazing performer," Fiona insisted. "You . . . can . . . do . . . this. Don't give up."

I love having friends. You know? I just really, really love having friends.

"I know you're right," I murmured.

"As usual," she said.

I heard a knock at my door. That was odd—Carlton was supposed to let me know if anyone was coming up. But it wasn't an ordinary day.

"I have to get the door," I said.

"And my break's over. Call me tonight, okay? Let me know how this turns out."

"Promise," I said, and hung up the phone. I trudged to the foyer. "Okay, Fritz, here I am, in living color," I announced, and swung open the door.

"Hey," said Jeb Razor.

I slammed the door. Oops. I opened it again.

"Sorry," I said. "I wasn't expecting—"

"Can I come in?" he asked.

"Of course." I stood back so he could enter. "Nobody's with you?"

"Nobody," he said. "I fired my posse."

"Didn't know you could fire a posse," I said. "Kind of like dismissing a mob or sacking a gang."

"It's been a tough year for the Crips, and we're going to have to lay some of you fellas off," he said, in a fake-bossy voice, and I laughed.

"Did you really fire them all?" I wanted to know.

"The ones who follow me around. It's a little embarrassing, and I think it's really time for me to grow

44

up and manage my own career. I still have a manager—but I want my style to be my own."

"That's really cool," I told him. Though I kind of hoped his own style included the fact that he dressed really awesomely and continued to look like a tasty piece of man-meat.

Clyde came trotting in and stood up, planting his front feet on Jeb like he was Clyde's first and only real owner. I'm telling you, this celebrity thing—it affects everyone.

"Hey, little pooch, you feeling better?" Jeb teased, crouching down to pet the dog's tummy, and Clyde wiggled his whole chubby body with pleasure.

"Not to be rude, but . . . what are you doing here?" I asked, sliding to the floor next to where they were playing. "And I have to warn you, you're on camera."

"I was worried about you," he said, giving the camera a little wave. "When you left, I figured you'd head home. I saw Fritz was waiting outside the bathroom and put two and two together. I wasn't sure I'd catch you, but—"

"Worried about me?" I made a face. "I mean, I was an idiot in there. I'd think you'd be annoyed. Irritated. Grossed out, maybe. But worried?"

He shrugged, his taut muscles showing in ripples through the thin workout shirt that stretched across his pecs.

"I could see Seth riding you from the first minute we started rehearsing," he said. "Before my band broke, we used to practice twenty-four/seven, and I got yelled at like crazy. I hated it. I could see he was taking out all his crap on you."

"Oh, I deserved it."

Jeb shook his head incredulously, and put a hand on my calf. (Yowza!) "Claire, nobody deserves that. He's just pissed because his show needs a boost of publicity, so he was forced to take on two rookies with no experience. And he couldn't yell at me, because I'd rehire my posse and have my agent tell him where to get off. You were the easiest target. He was being an asshole. You were right."

I swallowed. My self-loathing decreased by one and a half ounces. "You think?" I asked.

"I know." Make that three ounces.

I let out a breath of air. "But you had it all down perfectly," I said. "I really don't know the moves. I should have been able to follow along."

"Duh! Claire!" Jeb laughed, and his eyes crinkled up in this way that was totally and unmistakably adorable. I laughed too, nervously, though I didn't know why.

"Whaaat?" I asked.

"They give me tons of extra training! I have my own dance coach, my own trainer, my own private choreographer for anything I might have to improvise. I didn't know that stuff because of some inbred talent. I have a staff, for cripe's sake!"

"Are you kidding me?" I snapped. "You—that's not fair!" I gave him a shove, forgetting for a second that he was Jeb Razor and not, say, my best friend Peter. "I can't believe you!"

He was flat-out laughing now. I whapped him.

46

"Cut it out!" he said. "Come on! I was born with two left feet. I can't walk and chew gum at the same time! They only let me in the band because my voice changed early and I could hit the low notes."

"And grow a goatee," I teased him, laughing now too.

"Yeah, and grow a goatee," he agreed. "Plus, I happened to be trying out at the studio the day another guy quit, and they needed a warm body for the first round of publicity photos. I had some raw talent, and they whipped me into shape. But without a ton of extra work, I'm nothing but a nerdy dork. I had coke-bottle glasses—my eyes were so bad, I couldn't even wear contact lenses before they gave me laser surgery—and I spent my entire childhood with post-nasal drip from my horrible allergies. I used to sound like a frog when I sang. I know how it feels to not be able to do something the first time you see it. That's why I train around the clock. I'm totally scared to do things wrong." He looked up at the camera again. "And you can take that to *Entertainment Tonight*," he announced in its direction.

I sat quietly, thinking about it. "Thank you for telling me that," I said.

"Whatever." He shrugged. "Anyway, I was wondering—"

The phone rang, shattering the little bubble of peace that we'd created, me, Jeb, and Clyde. Clyde picked his head up and stared at the phone, beseeching it to stop jangling. I knew how he felt.

"I have to get that," I said. "I'm supposed to spend the afternoon getting chewed out."

"Wait, let me—"

"I'll get rid of them," I promised, and stood up to pick up the receiver. I hit the talk button and said, "Hello?"

"I can't believe you put me on hold," Haley fumed.

"I'm really sorry. It was just really confusing," I told her.

"You can't do this to the show," she ranted.

"I know. I feel stupid. I'd like to—"

"Don't be apologetic right now!" she yelled. "I'm really mad and I have to figure out what to do! Claire, I was counting on you to really commit to this, and I can't . . . I don't want you to look bad! But how else can the show go if you're going to act like a baby? I'm serious; you've got to pull it together and—"

I didn't hear the rest. Jeb had taken the phone.

"Hello," he said. It was a statement, not a greeting. "This is Jeb Razor. I want you to lay off of Claire."

I'm not sure what was going on, on the other end of the phone, but I think it involved sputtering, and possibly some hemming and hawing. "Yes, I'm serious," he said, grinning at me and tossing me a wink. "I want you to call Fritz and have him meet me at the Miracle Studios on Ninth Avenue and Forty-fifth Street. Claire's going to get the extra help she needs to catch up with the seasoned professionals she's working with. From my private dance coach, with me. Capeesh?"

Haley made a screechy noise that indicated relief and happiness.

"I'll take that as a yes," Jeb said, after holding the phone away from his ear during the screech. "Just

48

call Seth and tell him what I told you. And tell him I think he was an asshole, too, and if he acts like that again, I'm going to call the gossip columns and tell them he's into bestiality."

I heard another screech—this one slightly less pleased—and he chuckled. "Just pass that along. If you can't, I'll do it myself."

With that, he hung up the phone.

"I can't let you do that," I said.

"What?" he asked, incredulous.

"Your dance coach. Your trainer. I can't take that kind of charity." The words flew out of my mouth like Grace Marangello had said them herself.

"Charity? I need you in the show with me," Jeb scoffed. "I can't be the only rookie on that stage. And with your reality show, I'll get a wider audience to see I'm more than just a boy-band teddy bear."

I eyeballed him, unconvinced.

"Come on," he said. "I'm paying them anyway. And you need the boost. Come hang out. If you don't like it, then you can quit."

I stared at him for another long moment. I started to see past his celebrity veneer. Past the perfect features that looked like they were chiseled from tan-colored marble. Past the money and the fame and the "oooh-it's-Jeb-Razor!"-osity. I saw something even better-looking than his face, his body, even the smooth growl of his singing voice. I saw a guy, just a guy, with eyes so deep I could tumble into them and never hit bottom.

I hadn't felt that way in a long time. It felt warm. And it felt . . . exciting. Curtains up. You know?

"I really want to do this show," I said. It was the truest thing I've ever spoken.

"Then do it," he said. "Take the help and do it."

I felt my lips curl up in a smile as the light at the end of the tunnel expanded into bright, sunshiny hope.

"Okay," I said.

Somehow, in all this whirlwind, the TV show *Unscripted* had its premiere. My evenings were mostly taken up by those extra rehearsals, but Tina insisted that I slow down and take one evening to at least watch the first episode.

"Hey, if I can tell my bosses I can't stay late, you can come home by eight P.M.," she told me. To tell you the truth, I'm not used to having anyone lay down the law. That's my job. But somehow, Tina didn't get an argument out of me. Was it because I finally had an older sister? (In other words, was I getting a taste of my own senior-sibling medicine?)

Eh, maybe it was just her lawyerly training. She really can command some kind of power, I'm telling you.

Anyway, that night, we walked Clyde, picked up some takeout sushi, and then settled in to watch Episode One. As the opening montage played, I felt butterflies in my stomach. Isn't that funny, even after a year of being onscreen? When I saw my own face, I still got a little weird tummy-dip, like when you drive a car down a big hill too fast. Yoinks.

Of course, if I had butterflies, Tina had a beehive. I looked over and saw her negihamachi roll sitting untouched as she gazed at the screen with an expression that said, "Whatever's coming, it can't be good." I patted her delicate little shoulder.

"Don't worry," I said. "It's just a TV show."

"That's what my mom used to tell me when we watched *The Wizard of Oz* and I got scared of the flying monkeys," she said. "It's just a movie, it's just a movie. Except this time, it's me onscreen."

"But it's not," I told her. She fixed me with an utterly bemused expression.

"Look, if there's one thing I learned from being on last year's version of this show, it's that our lives are just raw material," I said. "They take what really happens, and they shape it to suit their storylines. The character on TV looks like you, sounds like you, acts sort of like you—but it's just a small piece of you, a piece that the directors and producers take and blow up into a character. The audience sits at home and thinks that's all there is to you, but you have to know there's more to it than that."

Tina shook her head. "But why do people do this?"

"What, be on reality shows?"

"Yeah."

I shrugged. "All different reasons. Look, you're on this one because we wanted a chance to get to know each other. And they're paying our rent. So, there're all kinds of payoffs."

The show started. The first ten minutes was just a wrap-up of last season—they showed my fight with Fiona (ugh), then a little friendship-development stuff.

"How did you guys deal with it?" Tina asked.

51

"How did you become friends with all these cameras on you?"

"We found ways to communicate that had nothing to do with them," I said. "When we were home, of course. And in school, we staked out the areas that were camera-free zones. Toward the end, Baxter showed us some baseball signs—some tricks for communicating in a kind of sign language. Look, you see that shot there? I scratch my nose, then I tug my hair? And I'm looking at Pete?"

"Yeah—" Tina said, dubiously.

"Well, that means 'I'm heading to the spot outside the locker room, meet me there after this class.' "

"You're kidding me."

"Nope. I've got to hand it to Baxter. I thought jocks were stupid, but they've got some pretty clever tricks up their sleeve."

On the TV, Pete and I were in the middle of our triumphant performance at Hamilton High's talent show/homecoming dance. That's what made the producers think I could do Broadway. So as embarrassing as it was to see myself in that funny gold lamé outfit, which matched Pete's vest and shimmered in the stagelights, I had to salute myself for having the nerve to do it.

Oh, who was I kidding. Of course I did it! I was born with nerve to spare!

"This is when I knew you had to be my sister," Tina smiled, as she watched the footage. "I was like, man, I don't know who my father ended up marrying, but his daughter ended up being so much like Mom."

52

"That's weird," I said, trying to unravel the knot of Freudian problems in what she was saying.

"I know, it's bizarre." She wrinkled her nose at me. "I just mean that my mom has so much spirit—not like me. I feel like a little mouse next to her sometimes. And you've got that same power. I guess your dad must attract bright lights."

"Huh. I mean, I'm sure you have spirit—just because you don't run around with a tambourine, like your mom, doesn't mean—oh, *blech*!" On the screen, Tina and I were meeting at the apartment, and Jeb was cleaning up Clyde's mess.

"Oh, you little scamp," I groaned, nudging Clyde with my toe.

"God, he couldn't care less that he's on TV," Tina pointed out, muffled by the pillow she was holding over her face, just peering over the top at the screen, utterly mortified by her own onscreen self. "That's probably a healthier attitude than the one us humans have—"

"Yeah, then again, he also couldn't care less that he piddled on the floor," I had to add.

"Good point." She scrunched down lower.

"We don't have to watch," I offered. "I mean, after this episode, I'm going to be at the theater when the show's on. It's not like we're going to have time to watch it every week. I promise, you'll forget about it—that is, until some stranger comes up to you in a store and starts talking to you about the show as if they know you."

"It's okay, I can watch," she insisted. "I mean, we

53

should do this. It's good! It's important. It's a bonding experience. It's—"

"Horrible," I stated, with a flat feeling of misery. There I was, calling my director an asshole. . . .

"Oh!" Tina snapped off the TV set. "Oh, gosh. That was that day they called me."

"Yeah." I chewed on my lip and picked at the wasabi on the takeout platter in front of me. "Jeez, sometimes I just hate myself."

"Don't say that!" Tina sat up and shook me. "I'm serious. I can't stand to hear women say that about themselves. My mom used to say it all the time, and it just seemed to spur her to act worse, because she already had no faith in her abilities."

"Jeez, I was just kidding," I joked.

"I know, you were saying it like you were kidding, but when you say stuff like that, you really—it's just not good. You can say 'I hate that I do that,' or better yet, 'I'm going to stop doing that,' but don't say you hate yourself."

"Okay, Oprah."

Tina rolled her eyes and laughed. "Fine, lecture over."

We turned the TV back on. I was done with my hissy. In fact, they were showing me doing some extra rehearsals, so I let it run, but turned the sound down.

"What do you mean, your mom didn't have faith in herself?" I asked. "I thought she did all this cool stuff, like making stained glass in Woodstock and teaching Yoga and having all these adventures. She sounds like she had a lot of courage, to do all that."

54

Tina shook her head. "My mom—she gets all enthusiastic about a new project, but the minute she hits something difficult, she gives up. It's like she's afraid that if she tries and fails, she'll feel worse than if she quits while she's ahead. It's so bizarre—and it's so annoying."

"I guess that's why you rebelled."

"You better believe it. It was all well and good for her to storm out of the ashram because she had a fight with the other receptionist, but someone had to make sure we had money for the rent. Usually it was me. I'd go to school, then spend four hours at a fricking factory job—it was such a grind, but I had to keep us going. My mom was so frail."

Looking at Tina, you'd think she was frail, too. But that lawyerly bossiness wasn't the only hint of steel in this little flower. She was stronger than anyone I knew. In the suburbs of Jersey, the biggest challenge most people face is the SATs, and let me tell you, that's a massive trauma for your average eleventh grader. Tina was my first hint that there was a wider world out there.

"I'll bet she's glad she had you," I said.

"Yeah, but I wasn't always glad I had her," she admitted. "It's horrible to say. I love her so much, it's crazy, but there were times when I got so tired of being the grownup. That's when I got angry at your dad. My dad." She shook her head. "Whoever. That's when I thought of how he used to come and play with me, and he seemed like this big ogre, this dark creature that had come into our lives and then left."

"Oh. Jeez," I said. "My dad? Ed Marangello?"

"I don't mean to speak badly about your dad—" she added, hastily.

"No, it's not that, it's, just that this great dark creature you're describing—it's strange to think my dad ever caused anyone heartbreak."

Tina just sat, regarding her maki combination. She reached over and took a piece, finally, and chewed thoughtfully.

"I found out recently that he sent as much money as he could while I was growing up. It wasn't much, but every little bit helped. I guess not knowing him has been worse than anything," she said. "My imagination ran wild. I mixed him up with fairy tale monsters, my friends' dads, Ted Hughes—"

"Ted who?"

"Husband of this poet Sylvia Plath—she wrote a poem called 'Daddy' that I used to think was all about my life. She said it was about her father, but it was also about her husband, and she called him 'the black man who bit my pretty red heart in two—' "

"Oh gosh."

She turned to me and laughed. "I was a little overwrought at times."

"You were angry," I said. "He abandoned you."

"I was too busy to think about it, really," she said, with a wave of her hand that I didn't believe for a second.

"Well, I think you're really strong," I said. "And I think you'll find out, my dad's hardly a fascist. He's Italian, and—well, he did ground me for a week when I got my ears pierced—"

56

Tina laughed. "I knooooow, I know the real Ed Marangello has nothing to do with the ogre I imagined. Right now, I'm not worried about him—I'm just psyched to get to know you. And the rest of the kids, when we have a chance."

"Oh, I'm definitely the best one," I stated. "I mean, once you've met me, you don't need to meet the rest of them. It's a letdown."

"Aaah, I can see I didn't have to worry about keeping your self-esteem up," Tina teased.

"You're right. I can't believe I said that. I hate myself," I cracked up, and she thumped me with a pillow.

We looked up. The first episode of *Unscripted* was over, and we'd barely watched it. "See?" I said. "I told you it was no big deal."

Tina popped a piece of sushi in her mouth. "Maybe you're right," she said. "Anyway, it's out there now—nothing I can do. I'll just stay away from shopping in any stores till it's all over, and I'll be fine."

Oh yeah. I wish it really were that easy.

E-MAIL
TO: <Fiona>; <Peter>
FROM: <Inbox, Claire Marangello>
SUBJECT: My aching bones!
BODY: Guys, I've never worked so hard in my life! Yikes! Jeb's trainer is a monster. My legs feel like spaghetti. All those hours at the studio were nothing compared to the hours I'm logging now. I didn't know the human body could do what mine's doing, but I love it. Maybe I'm even get-

ting better. You think that's possible? Crap, I'm late for rehearsal already.
SENT: JUNE 25, 6:05 A.M.
ARCHIVED IN SENT MAIL FOLDER

E-MAIL
To: <Inbox, Claire Marangello>
From: <Fiona>
CC: <Peter>
SUBJECT: Re: My aching bones!
BODY: We know you can do it! I'm so glad you stayed. Jeez, you sounded like you were going to give up for a second there. Of course you are getting better, you idiot. P.S. Baxter says hi. Guess where we went? To see Bon Jovi at the Meadowlands. I am so Jersey. Help. lovelovelove feee
RECEIVED: JUNE 26, 7:48 A.M.
ARCHIVED IN BEST BUDDIES FOLDER

E-MAIL
To: <Inbox, Claire Marangello>
From: <Peter>
CC: <Fiona>
SUBJECT: You go, girl!
BODY: Yeah, what Fiona said! I miss you, though. But I don't want to see your face until you've won a Tony award. I mean it, diva. Now get back to that studio and work. Oh, snap! Claire's yelling at me that we've got to leave now or we'll get stuck in Turnpike traffic on the way to Hurricane Harbor. I really do miss you, baby-

cakes. Don't tell Fee, but she's not as much of a roller coaster as you. So sensible, these city girls. Write again soon. Kisses, P

RECEIVED: June 26, 8:05 A.M.

ARCHIVED IN BEST BUDDIES FOLDER

E-MAIL:

From: <Joey>

To: <Inbox, Claire Marangello>

SUBJECT: Hey, what's up, slick? Surprised to hear from me? I'm in study hall. I saw you in the first episode. You looked good. I mean, you looked really good. Well, you always did. Ha, ha—sorry if you don't want to hear that from me. But you know you always have a special place in my pants—I mean heart. Ha, ha, ha. Seriously, though, do you think I could come see you in the big city? We always said we'd go walking down theater row and you'd show me what all the excitement was about. Well, I think I'd like to see for myself. If I saw that and I held your hand I think I'd feel like the whole world was just right. Hope I'll hear from you soon. You looked hot, for real, really beautiful. You were always beautiful to me. When you were my little star. Bye, now.

RECEIVED: June 26, 12:42 P.M.

DELETED BY READER

Chapter Four

"Come on, Fritz."

"I'm not supposed to do that!"

"I know that, but come on."

"Claire!"

"Friiitz! Just let me see. I want to know if I'm doing better. You know? Give a girl a break."

We were standing in the dank downstairs area of my rehearsal studio. Well, Jeb's rehearsal studio. The one he rented. The place was . . . what's the word? Redolent. It was redolent with theater history. Old-time tap-dancers used this place as their home base. Sometimes I feel like I can still hear them, creating rhythm with their feet, challenging each other, not bothering with an audience. Just dancing for the joy of it. One time I actually saw Savion Glover walking out with a tall guy, sad eyes, light-brown skin, who I think I saw in a movie once. They walked like their bodies were the most comfortable clothes they'd ever worn.

It smells like wood and resin and sweaty workout

clothes, but not stinky sweaty. Worky sweaty. It's hard to explain. The light is pale, because the sun has to go through thick panes of dirty glass. It's dusty. My allergies kick up sometimes—so do Jeb's, and he turned me on to some new medicine to fight the sniffles—but I don't care. This place is heaven to me.

But there's no point being in heaven if you're just going to get kicked out for playing the harp badly. Right? I had to know if this past week of work was paying off. I'd been getting up at 5 A.M. to squeeze in extra practice, and every time our regular rehearsals left a gap—like when Seth was concentrating on the other principles—I would schedule more sessions. It was harder than hard: I'd just finished a grueling rehearsal during which my muscles actually trembled and felt like they were going to give out. But I pushed through. And I wanted a payoff before Seth saw me in rehearsal again.

"Just a peek," I wheedled.

Fritz relented, rewound his tape, and let me look in the viewfinder at myself.

At first all I could see was that my butt looked kind of big, considering how hard I'd been working. Then that my hair looked frizzy and my ponytail was off-kilter (God, wasn't there a giant mirror in that studio?). But then I stepped back (in my head, obvie, or I wouldn't be able to see the viewfinder) and realized that the girl working it on that tape was about fifty times better than the one who had stumbled through rehearsal a week earlier. Maybe a hundred times. She looked professional. She looked confident. And she looked like she was full of joy because she could dance like that.

And that girl was me. I couldn't believe it.

I handed Fritz back his camera and tried to twist my mouth so it wouldn't burst into the wide grin it wanted to. I didn't want to seem conceited, but I was proud of myself. Fritz rewound the tape back to where it was, and put it back to his face.

"You've gotten a lot better," he said. "You should be proud."

"Thanks," I said. Then the red record-light came on and I pushed open the door to head home. It was dinnertime, and I'd barely seen Tina all week.

"Yowch," I yelped. A long, hot shower had barely made my muscles stop aching, and as I settled my feet into their Epsom salt bath, the water scalded the blisters that were slowly but surely turning into the calluses I needed to protect myself. It hurt, but less than the night before, and less than the night before that.

Clyde padded over and sniffed curiously at the bubbling water of the footbath I'd plugged into the outlet.

"Hey, get away from there," I ordered. "Your water's over there. Or in the toilet. This is bad for you."

He looked at me, then decided I was telling the truth. He lumbered up onto the couch next to me and put his fat head in my lap with a massive sigh.

"I know, buddy," I told him. "I'll tell you, cotton pajamas have never felt so good. I'm going to wear them to everything that's not a rehearsal for the rest of my life."

"Urr?" he asked me.

"Even the Tonys, yeah. And the Oscars, when they have me in the movie of the play. Even in my *Oprah* interview. What do you think she'd say if I showed up in Nick and Nora striped jammie-bottoms with a matching tank top?

He grunted.

"Me too." I stared at the ceiling, too tired to order food. I wanted to stay awake to hang out with Tina, but it was getting harder by the minute. Her job was too fricking demanding. She was never home. It was a waste of money for her to have an apartment at all. The way that firm worked her, she should have slept in the office-supply closet.

"Hello?" I heard her come in the front door.

"Tina!" I sat up, and Clyde ran to greet her. "Hey, what's up?"

"Heeey," she said dubiously, eyeballing Fritz. He was sitting on the kitchen counter, training the camera on Clyde. He raised it till he met her irritated gaze, then started back like he'd been burned.

"Oops! Sorry," he said. "Just shooting a little B reel. I'm heading out now." He shut his camera off, shoved it into the bag, and gave me a wave. "See you tomorrow," he said.

"Are you okay?" I asked. "You seem a little—"

Tina gave a quick shake of her head, then glanced up at the stationary camera mounted in the corner of the living room. We were still on. I looked out at the fire escape. She nodded. I tugged some thick slouchy socks onto my feet, put the cover on my foot-bath (no, Clyde, it's the toilet for you), and climbed out the window onto the rickety metal platform outside.

Tina yanked on some sweatpants, then hiked up her skirt so she could make the trip, too. The effect was pretty hilarious: high-powered lawyer in red suit, sweatpants, and panty hose. I would have laughed if she didn't look so panicked and upset.

"What's going on?" I asked.

Tina sighed, and glanced back in the window as if she were afraid the camera would follow her out.

"The head of my firm saw my appearance on your show when it premiered this week," she said.

"Oh, no. He didn't like it?" I asked. God! Why had I let her be dragged into this?

"No, that's the problem," she said. "He liked it. A lot. Said he didn't realize he had such a photogenic associate at the firm. He wants to capitalize on the publicity."

"I don't get it," I said.

"He wants me to go into the courtroom and try a case in front of a judge and jury," she blurted out, like she'd just admitted that she was a murderer.

"But that's great!" I said. "You need courtroom experience if you're going to make partner, right?"

"Ugh, Claire, you don't understand," she told me. "I didn't go into law to be a grandstanding blowhard. I just like rules and words and documents. They're solid. They make sense. Not like people. People are unpredictable; they do whatever they want. In the law, nothing happens without a precedent, and nothing changes too quickly. That's why I'm in this. So what if I don't make partner? I don't care about that. I can't go in front of all those people and talk. I'm going to blow it if they don't let me off the hook."

"Tina! Come on!" I tried to give her the same pep talk that Fiona had given me. "You're a talented lawyer. You can't let this nervousness about speaking in public throw you off—"

"I'm not like you!" she snapped. "I can't do it! I don't want to do it! Dammit, I don't want to be noticed, I don't want attention, I don't want complication. I just want to be left alone."

As if cued by an offstage sound engineer, the phone began ringing inside the apartment. Tina pushed the window open wider to listen. It rang four times, and then the machine picked up.

"Hi, it's us; leave a message," my voice sang out.

"Hey. It's Jonah," a forlorn voice said. "I know you, uh, I know you don't want to talk for whatever reason. I mean, you're busy; that's probably why you're not calling me back. At least I hope that's why. Uh, this message is for Tina. If you're screening this, pick up. . . . Well, I guess you're not screening. Or you're not . . . Okay, so give me a call."

It clicked off. Then it rang again, just twice this time, before the machine picked up. "Hey! It's Jonah. I'm calling for Claire. Can you tell your sister to give me a call?" Pause, pause, pause. "I figured it was worth a shot."

He hung up. Tina looked devastated, but she didn't make a move to go inside, not even when it rang a third time.

"Clyde, old pal," Jonah said. "I'd take you for a walk, buddy, but I don't have a key. Tell that old lady of yours that there's a man out here who'd like to see her sometime. Anytime. Okay? Okay. Well. So . . . bye. Call me. Bye."

He hung up, and this time the phone stayed silent. Tina's forehead was leaning against the glass of the window. She was sitting cross-legged, the slats of the fire escape probably making red stripes on her pale legs. She looked tired, and not in the way I felt tired— the tired of hard work done well. She looked exhausted, like life was wringing her dry.

"You gonna call him?" I asked.

She picked up her head and seemed to think about it. Then she fixed me with a level, even stare.

"No complications," she said, and climbed back in the window.

Yikes. As I followed her into the apartment, I wondered if this was my fault. By just showing up—invading her life, forcing her to be on television, exposing her like this—had I driven her into this emotional shell? Or was she always like this? I had no way of knowing. And there didn't seem to be anything I could do or say to make it better.

Together, silently, we pulled some frozen dinners out of the freezer and warmed them up in the microwave. Then we sat side by side and ate them at the counter.

"It's good," I said.

"Mmm. Not bad," she told me.

It was pretty silent. Not good, not bad, but just quiet. Clyde got a lot of scraps—we couldn't help ourselves. I just tried to be near my sister without bothering her.

The buzzer rang, startling us both.

"Jeb is here," Carlton told us. "With some cameras."

"What? Tell him to go home," I said. "I'm in my pajamas; I'm done for the night."

"I've got a surprise," Jeb said.

Tina waved at me, like, "It's okay, have him come up." "I'm going to change and take the dog out," she said. "It's fine."

I gave Carlton the go-ahead, then looked down at my schlubby outfit. Well, if you drop in on a girl, you've got to pay the price, and seeing me in my jammies was quite a penance.

"I'm sorry about the cameras, but they caught up with me," Jeb said. "Go get your fanciest outfit. We're going out."

"Jeb! It's Monday night," I scolded him.

"Monday's the new Friday," he told me. "Come on. Doll yourself up. You deserve a night out after the work you put in this past week. Don't you?"

Well . . . yes, I did. After the week of grueling training, repetitive dance moves, and sore hamstrings, I did deserve to celebrate. I pursed my lips and pretended to consider it: a night out in Manhattan with the hottest star in the pop-culture galaxy? Yes, please!

"Okay. Give me twenty minutes," I said.

"You've got ten," he said.

"You just made it a half hour."

Jeb laughed, and Tina ducked her head in greeting as she passed us, holding Clyde on his leash. I ran to the bathroom to drown my hair in Frizz-Ease.

Chapter Five

You know how Cinderella got picked up in a pump-kin coach and whisked off to a magical night at the ball?

Well, Cinderella's an amateur.

The night I had with Jeb was like . . . I mean, let's start with the fact that if we'd done nothing but hold hands at the mall, we would have had a fantastic time. Just being with him sets off fireworks in my chest—he makes me feel nervous without the upset stomach, which turns out to be a really nice feeling.

Ugh, I know I sound corny. But it's totally different when you're crushing on a guy who's crushing on you back. All of a sudden the corniest of songs on the radio make sense: Dammit, Celine Dion is right; I could touch the moonlight! My heart is shooting stars! And ohmigod, I really am walking on air!

So add to that the fact that me and Jeb were not holding hands at the mall. No, sirree. This evening wasn't just cloud nine. It was stratospheric. Cloud nine billion.

Okay, I'll start at the beginning. The pre-beginning, even. I ran to my closet and for once I was glad that I'm an inveterate over-packer. When I was throwing things into my suitcase—okay, suitcases—for the ride into the city for the summer, my little sister Angela sat on my bed and made fun of me: "What are you going to do with all these clothes?" she wanted to know. "You're going to be in sweatpants and tights all day, every day, and then you're going to be in costume."

"You never know," I told her, and she laughed. Well, check it out, Angela! A rock-star knocked on my door and asked me out on an impromptu date. And voilà, here's my junior prom dress!

This dress was so beautiful, I'd decided to give it a name: Fifi. As in, "Come on, Fifi, let's go to the prom!" "Poor Fifi, she only gets one big night out." "Me and Fifi had a great time with you, Pete." I found her when Fiona dragged me into the city to shop, complaining that everybody looked "too Jersey," and she just wanted to show me what else was out there. We went to a lot of small boutiques, but Fifi was from a big designer with a boutique in SoHo—Max Azria— and she just called out to me.

I slipped Fifi on, my skin still flushed from the hot shower, and immediately felt ready for a night out on the town. Fifi was a deep coral pink, almost red— the color of lips swollen from too much kissing. She had a straight white slip, and laid over it was this deep-hued chiffon, embroidered with tiny flowers from the thin straps down the V neck, at the waist, and in two lines down the front. It flowed out at my calves in a little bell shape. It's exquisite, like the Valentino gown that Cate Blanchett wore to the Oscars. I paired Fifi with matching stilettos that had satin straps which tied around the ankle (like toe shoes, but in a deeper color that matched the dress), and a couple of strips of duct tape, since I couldn't wear a bra with those little straps.

I tottered out to the living room so I could look at myself in the mirror. Not bad. A little dramatic, a little flashy—but hey, who are we talking about here? And anyway, I was going out with Jeb Razor. I wanted everyone to notice me.

Tina came back from walking Clyde just as I finished my inspection. "They're waiting—ohhhh!" She stood and gazed at me, her hand to her heart as if she were about to pledge allegiance to me.

"Is this OK? Too over-the-top?" I asked, stricken.

"You look beautiful. Like Nicole Kidman," she said.

"If she was attacked by an Afro and lost," I pointed out.

"But your style—so feminine, so delicate. Oh, you look beautiful. I don't know what I expected, something more like Jennifer Lopez—"

"I do have a romantic side," I pointed out. "And maybe it's my inner Grace rearing her head, but I think baring too much belly is tacky."

"Wait, wait just a second," she said, handing me Clyde's leash and leaving me standing in the living room, the dog staring worshipfully up at me (and probably eyeing my shoes as a possible place to pee). I unclasped his leash and straightened up just as she came back out, holding something on a silver chain.

"I want you to wear this tonight," she said. "My mother gave it to me. A friend of hers designed it, and the colors—it just goes so well."

Now it was my turn to pledge allegiance. "Oh, Tina, I couldn't—what if I lose it?"

"You won't lose it. It'll bring you luck. Just try it."

She turned me toward the mirror and stood behind me, gently stretching the chain along my collarbone, then clasping it around my neck. She peered over my shoulder as it hit my skin. It was a delicate flower, in pale pinks and white and purples that perfectly complemented the dress without competing for attention—it was just a simple bit of sparkle, above my cleavage, below my face, that caught the eye just ever so slightly. It was perfect.

"Your mom has amazing taste," I said.

"She loves beautiful things," Tina answered. "She'd pass out if she saw you now."

I stared at the teeny blossom, sitting on the warm skin of my breastbone, and tried to imagine the free spirit who'd bought it. I tried to imagine my father with her, holding her hand and looking at their baby. I wondered if I showed this to my dad, if he'd recognize it as something his old love would choose, or if all that was so old and far away that it would just be an ordinary flower on a silver rope. I thought of it resting around my neck, then resting around the neck of this woman, my older sister, and a stranger. Except not. Tina'd never be a stranger again.

I turned to face her. I thought, maybe, that I saw a little bit of my father in her. Not in the color of the eyes, but in their shape, and maybe she looked like me a little more than I'd thought. "Thank you," I said, hugging her tight. She crushed me to her, then pulled back to grab my upper arms and look at me one more time.

"So exciting!" she peeped.

"Come with us!" I blurted out. I know, what a weird impulse! What would Jeb say if I showed up with a chaperone? But at that moment, I just didn't want to let her go.

"On your date? You're crazy!" she laughed. "Have a wonderful time."

"I want you to have fun, too." I did. She looked so tired, in her shorts and sneakers. She deserved a night out more than I did.

"I will. Me and Clyde will watch some TiVo. I have to catch up with *Carnivale*, you know."

I sighed. "Someday, I'm going to make you go out for real—"

"Someday. But tonight, you're going out with Jeb Razor. In a limo."

"In a—" I ran to the window, but it looked down on the wrong stretch of street. "Are you serious?"

"Get out of here!" she ordered. "Go see for yourself!" Clyde barked, unused to her commanding tone. I grabbed my feathery clutch bag (shut up, it's fabulous!) and kissed her on the cheek, then ran out the door.

Downstairs, Jeb was chatting with Carlton and actually looking a little nervous. When he saw me, though, he gave me a wide smile that told me Fifi was a hit. After he handed me a gorgeous bouquet of red roses, he took my hand and led me through the cool marble of my lobby, out to—indeed—a waiting limousine. Black, thank goodness—white would be so prom night. We settled into the buttery leather seats and I felt the soothing coolness of the AC on my feverish, nervous skin. He slid in next to me, and I can tell you exactly where we were touching: Our knees rested lightly together, and his left arm and my right arm were, like, connected. He put a hand on my knee, not in a gross way, but, just as though he was saying hi, and I felt like he'd leave a handprint from how intensely my skin responded to his touch.

If you've seen any of Jeb's band's videos, you know that they can dress kind of funny sometimes. Flashy stuff that looks great when they're dancing, but would be kind of weird just to walk around on the street in. Well, I'm happy to report that Jeb knows how to dress. I believe I've mentioned that his entire body is muscled, but I'll say it again: Six-pack, pecs, and biceps, all in perfect shape. And the boy is tall. The way he had his legs kind of stretched out in front of him was so cute. He was wearing these Italian jeans that fit him to a tee. I mean, I know you're thinking, "Jeans? For a fancy night out?" But trust me, these were fancy jeans. Paired with a button-down casual black silk shirt, it all came together really nicely. I admired him when he wasn't looking. And when he was. It was all I could do not to just melt into a puddle of longing when his eyes met mine.

"So where are we going?" I asked.

"Just wait," he said.

First stop was the Empire State Building. Call me a

weirdo, but in all those years of seeing it across the Hudson River, I'd never taken the elevator up to the top. I heard excited whispers around us—there wasn't much of a crowd, but a couple of people recognized Jeb, and I knew they were wondering who I was, too. Maybe they'd even seen the show. My heart beat with a weird sort of excitement, like I was doing something slightly naughty just by being recognized, and I reminded myself to be polite and gracious if anyone said anything. But they didn't. Maybe because of Fritz and his ever-present camera, or maybe because they were just too nervous. I could feel their eyes, though. Almost as if they were brushing my skin.

Once we switched elevators and rode to the very top, we walked through the inner lobby, with its Art Deco style and tacky gift shop, and opened the glass doors to the night air. The city looked like a fairy village, all lined-up lights and tiny cars. We ran around the observation deck, giggling like kids in the night air. I put a quarter in one of the big metal binoculars and swung it around, looking at whatever.

"I can't see anything through this thing," I complained.

He came up behind me and guided me to a spot somewhere to the east. "See that clock tower?" he asked me. I nodded, because his breath in my ear rendered me totally unable to speak. "That's Brooklyn. Drive past that about eighty blocks down Fourth Avenue, and you'll get to Bay Ridge."

"What's there?" I asked.

"My parents," he said.

"You're from Brooklyn?" I turned around and looked up at him. "You don't have an accent."

"Yeah, they kinda made sure of that." He shrugged, rolling his eyes. "Don't worry; it still comes out when I'm tired, angry, or talking to my parents."

"I'd love to hear that." I laughed.

He gave me a long look. I thought maybe he was going to kiss me, but he didn't. Oh, wait! He did! He kissed me right there on top of the Empire State Building. I felt his lips against mine and I hoped I was kissing back the right way. Joey's the only person I've kissed for so long that I wasn't sure—but it was short, you know, no tongue, so I didn't have to do much. I gulped, and when he pulled back, grinning at me, I felt like I didn't know what to say.

"I uh . . . I feel like Meg Ryan in *Sleepless in Seattle*," I said. Ugh! Stupid! Dork!

Jeb laughed. "Oh yeah? Well I feel like King Kong. In *King Kong*."

Mortified, I followed him to the elevator, and we went back down to the limo.

"Now what?" I asked. "The Statue of Liberty? Maybe the Stock Exchange?"

"No, the tourist portion of the evening's over," he said. "I want to show you a place I love."

We drove downtown to the West Village. That's the old part of Manhattan, where the streets bust out of the even, methodical grid of Midtown, and start meandering off on weird one-way side streets that are pretty impossible to find your way around. The buildings are smaller: no skyscrapers, just a lot of short, charming old brick brownstones. We pulled up in front of one, and the door opened.

"Is this someone's house?" I asked.

"No. This is Ye Waverly Inn," he told me.

Sure enough, we walked in a garden-level door to find a softly lit, candle-studded room. There was a fireplace with a fire crackling in it (and the AC up full blast, to offset the charming heat). The place was filled with tables, but only one was made up. For two. I turned to Fritz and bugged my eyes out.

"Are you getting all this?" I asked through gritted teeth. His camera went up and down in a nod, and I strolled across the room, on my totteringly high heels, and allowed a friendly, neatly dressed waiter to guide me into a seat.

"I'm thinking duck," Jeb said.

"Why, did someone throw something at me?" I asked.

He peeked over the top of his menu. "Funny." He smirked. "What do you like?"

You! I screamed inside my head.

"Chicken?" I said.

"Great. I'll get the duck, you get the chicken, and we'll switch off halfway through."

"A fowl feast," the waiter said, and took the menus with a neat snap of his wrist.

"He reminds me of my friend Peter," I said as we were left alone (sorta, if you didn't count Fritz).

Jeb poured me some Perrier. "I remember him from the show," he said. "Seems like a nice guy. You guys were friends from when you were a kid?"

"A teeny-tiny kid," I told him, and launched into

the very famous (in Hamilton) story of how Peter and I were enrolled in the same toddler swimming class at the Paine Park pool.

"We had the same water wings," I told him. "And neither one of us would take them off. They weren't allowed, but we banded together. Maybe the teacher could have handled one of us, but there was no way she could battle the Peter-and-Claire-Monster. By the end of the class she'd talked us into at least letting the air out of them. We'd splash around fearlessly as long as we had these empty water wings on our arms, but take them off and we'd sink like a couple of stones."

Jeb laughed. "We had this pool program at the Y, but nobody wanted to go in that water after we saw the sign that said, 'Don't pee in the pool.' We realized that if people had to be told not to pee, who knew what else was going on?"

From there, the conversation just rolled. I had no sense of how long it went on. Jeb's stories were all so funny, and he kept asking for more of mine. And then we got onto other sports stuff, other camp stories, all kinds of growing-up tales. I mean, I don't know what we were talking about, but somehow the food showed up and the bottle emptied and another one came—I wanted a glass of wine, but try sneaking in an underage drink when you're on national TV; it's just not going to happen. It's just as well. I felt intoxicated anyway.

Two matching crème brûlées later, we stumbled back out into the soft, warm night air.

"I'm so full," I complained.

"Want to walk around a little?" Jeb asked. "Work it off?"

"I think my feet can take it," I said. "I know they can. I'm a dancer, dammit!"

Make a mental note of this: There is nothing stranger than strolling hand in hand down a darkened city street, passing couples with their small poofy dogs, while a limo tails behind you and a camera guy walks backward in front of you. Weird, weird, but who cared? When Jeb pulled me into him again, and leaned me against a metal fence to smooch me for real, I don't think I would have noticed if there were a police spotlight on us and the entire lineup of the Rolling Stones playing the opening chords of "Satisfaction" across the street. There was nothing in the world but the dipping feeling in my stomach, my hands finding the muscles of his arms through his soft shirt, and the warm, slidey feeling of Jeb's tongue meeting mine somewhere in the warm cave of our two mouths. I had to remember to keep breathing, and it was all I could do to keep my breaths long and even: I was trembling.

Maybe we kissed for a minute, maybe for an hour. I know I had time to slip my hands from his arms, to his shoulders to his chest, luxuriating in the feeling of his solid frame beneath my fingers.

"That was such a fantastic dinner," I whispered between kisses. "Thank you."

"I didn't even taste it," he whispered. "Was it good?"

"The best," I murmured.

He smiled into another kiss, and our teeth knocked

briefly against each other. It made me laugh, and we came apart, still holding hands but feeling like a warm blanket was around the two of us.

"Come on, back in the car," Jeb said as the limo pulled up from its post five feet behind us.

"Where to now?" I asked.

"Something kooky!" he promised.

We drove straight across town on the big, wide street called Houston Street. Here's a word of advice: When you're in a car with a cute guy who was born in New York City, do not look out the window and say "Oh, this is Houston Street," like you know what it is, and pronounce it "Hyoo-stun," like the city in Texas. Why? Because he'll crack up laughing at you. And why is that? Because it turns out that in New York City, they pronounce that street "House-ton," as in "House of Pain," and they completely forget that there's another way to pronounce it in the rest of the country.

I'm not saying that's what I did; I'm just saying . . . okay, that's what I did.

Anyway, we cruised across town to Second Avenue and Second Street, which sounds like the almost-center of the universe, doesn't it?

"Wow, the East Village," I said, peering out the window. "Is that a punk rocker?" A kid walked past us wearing plaid pants with long, sorta suspendery-looking straps hanging from them, a black T-shirt ripped at the sleeves, and enough piercings to set off every alarm at Newark Airport.

"Possibly a punk rocker, or just a really devoted Avril Lavigne fan," Jeb cracked, and I laughed. The fact is, the East Village is where all the cool kids congregate to dress different from everyone else, but exactly like each other. They look good, though. I like purple hair. On other people.

I stepped out of the limo, which looked kind of weird in this area of self-consciously downscale everything. Not that I noticed. There was a cute little coffee shop, up one (smelly and uneven) flight of stairs, with groovy wall sconces and a purple velvet couch and chairs, all arranged to look out the big glassed-in windows along two walls.

"What, everyone likes the view of this blank white building?" I asked, as we settled in among Goth-looking girls in red leather pants (summer, may I remind you; it was summer!) and guys in T-shirts bearing seventies-era advertising icons (we were sandwiched between Mr. Bubble and the Trix rabbit). Suddenly the sound system crackled to life, and groovy sixties music started blasting through. Like, girl groups. Motown. You know, oldies.

I looked at Jeb—I don't know what I was expecting him to say—and saw that he was looking out the window. His eyes met mine for a second, and then he nodded toward the glass; I turned to look outside, and saw that on the big blank wall across the street, a video to the music was playing—three black girls with bouffant hairdos, wearing identical white dresses with poofy skirts, white gloves, and pale stiletto heels, bouncing down the street and singing the song we were hearing. A couple of the Goth girls sang along as they sipped their iced decaf mocha latte espressos. It was like watching MTV from a Folgers-scented time capsule.

"This is so wild," I murmured. "They made videos back then?"

"Oh, yeah. They had these video jukeboxes," Jeb answered, his eyes glued to the yesteryear women sashaying back and forth across the street in the black-and-white image outside the window. "Amazing marketing idea. Way before its time. Thank goodness someone dug these up and preserved them. Can you imagine if they'd been lost?"

"Well, it's not like they're 2 Hot 4 U videos," I whispered, keeping the name of his boy group on the down-low, just in case anyone was listening to us (they were already being remarkably nonchalant about the presence of Fritz).

Jeb snorted, and then muttered under his breath so the microphone wouldn't pick up on it, "Our stupid videos aren't even in the same league as these. A bunch of fake pretty boys pretending to be Ken dolls, on an overproduced soundstage with CGI Barbies inserted next to us. Forget it. These videos are ten times simpler, and about a thousand times better."

"You sure are hard on yourself," I admonished him. "For a piece-of-crap band, you guys pull in some big bucks. Somebody's got to think you're decent."

"Sure, the same preteen girls who wet their pants over *NSync last year, and who are gonna go crazy over the new *American Idol* next year. No offense," he said, nodding in my direction.

"I did have a bit of a thing for the Backstreet Boys,"

I admitted. "But that's not the point. The point is—Oh! Is that Diana Ross? Look at her giant hair!"

After about seven songs, the videos gave way to *The Wizard of Oz*. The Technicolor images appeared slightly blurry on the wall outside, and the sound wasn't the actual sound track, but that Pink Floyd album, *Dark Side of the Moon*.

"My dad used to listen to this," I said. "Why are they playing it now?"

"Urban legend," Jeb said. "People say if you play this album along with this movie, it matches up in weird and bizarre ways. Personally, I think it's bull, but it's fun to watch anyway."

The mellow, old-school music made me feel a little blurry around the edges, despite the coffee and the sight of a twenty-foot-tall Judy Garland. The room exploded in alarm-clock sounds just as Miss Gulch arrived on screen; it was a perfect example of the sound track lining up to the movie.

"Hey, it works," I said. "But this song is annoying."

"I'd say that's our cue to take off," Jeb said, grabbing my hand again and taking me back down to the limo.

"Now what?" I asked, bouncing up and down. "Where are we going? Uptown? Downtown? What's the next stop?"

"The best thing of all," Jeb said. "Wait till you see. You think Motown videos were good, the night's about to get a whole lot better."

Better? I was already riding around on a cloud, limo or no limo. This had to be the funnest night of my life. Yes, indeed, before this night, the most fun I ever

85

had was when my parents lost me at Disneyland and I got to hang out with the uncostumed Mickey and Minnie and eat all the cotton candy I wanted; this beat that by about twenty nautical miles.

We headed uptown—back to Midtown, near our theater and my apartment. Somewhere around Twenty-third Street, Jeb had a very romantic sneeze-attack.

"Oh man, I hate my allergies," he complained.

"What's that stuff you gave me? Flonase?" I asked. "It worked like a charm."

"I know, I'm due for a shot of it," he admitted, honking into a hankie. "Do you mind?" he asked Fritz, who concentrated on the view out the window as Jeb stuck the bottle up his nose and sniffed.

"This stuff saves my life," he said. "I'm totally crippled without it."

He tucked it away, thank goodness—adenoids are not my idea of sexy—and we finally pulled up to a sort of nondescript, hotel-looking building with a big blue awning.

"This looks boring," I commented, reading the awning. "The Supper Club? Are we going to meet my aunt Phyllis for tea?"

"Oh, man, are you going to feel stupid that you said this place looked boring." Jeb snickered. "Come on; get your butt out of the limo."

I rolled my eyes at him and let Fritz slip out first, then followed him, standing on the sidewalk and feeling like I'd had a full night already. It was well after ten P.M. and we did have rehearsal in the morning.

"You know I can't drink, right?" I said to Jeb. "I don't even have a fake ID. So if we're here for a nightcap—"

"We're not here to drink," he told me. "We're here to see some of the greatest stars on Broadway let loose."

We walked through a very grand-looking dining room and then up some thickly carpeted stairs to a room labeled the King Kong Room. Gilded fixtures adorned the walls, but there were also big metal palm trees, and a huge mural of the aforementioned giant gorilla with Fay Wray stretching across one wall. The room was crowded with handsome men and gorgeous women milling around with drinks, screaming with laughter, and basically having the time of their lives. A grand piano sat at one end of the room, bathed in a spotlight, with a microphone and a stool settled nearby.

"Ohmigod," I said. "Is that Bernadette Peters? Are we here to see her sing?"

"Her and everyone else," Jeb told me. "Don't you recognize any of the other people in this room?"

I scanned the place, and sure enough, familiar faces started to pop out of the dim light like headlights on a dark highway. Some of them I knew only from the posters outside their theaters. Some were stars I'd known from stage and from the movies. And they were all here. . . . What was going on? I turned back to Jeb with giant question marks popping out of my eyes, but he just grinned.

A blond guy in a sharp black suit came out and picked up the mike as another guy sat at the piano.

"Hello, I'm Jim Caruso," he announced, as the piano player started vamping. "Welcome to the King Kong Room's cast party. Let's be nice, now, and take turns, all right? I see the cast of *Urban Cowboy* just shuffled in, and oh, my, it's a star-studded evening. First up, in fact, is a screen legend, so please put your lips together and whistle for Miss Lauren Bacall!"

I gasped and almost fell backward. The movie star from the forties and fifties came strutting onto the little stage, sat on the stool, and proceeded to warble her way through "Let's Misbehave." It was so surreal, I'm telling you, like seeing a spaceship land in the middle of the Short Hills Mall. As soon as she finished, Nathan Lane—you know, the guy from *The Birdcage* and *The Producers*—bounded into the spot she vacated, and belted out the best version of "I Am What I Am" I'd ever heard. It was, like, so emotional and powerful, even though it was from a fun show, *La Cage Aux Folles* (I saw it when I was ten and insisted on wearing a feather boa to school for a month afterward).

"Oh, God! Now who's this?" I asked, as a beautiful, willowy blond woman strode up.

"That's Kristin Chenoweth," Jeb whispered back. "You know who she is. She played Glinda in the original cast of *Wicked*."

I gasped. Of course. She was so larger-than-life onstage that it hadn't occurred to me that she could walk around like a regular person. And she brought the house down with "Gee, Officer Krupke," a goofy song from *West Side Story*. It's usually sung by a bunch of rowdy guys, and she made it sound so funny! I never heard such a big noise from such a petite person!

"This is so wild," I said, totally transfixed on the little wooden stool onstage. "It's like the best karaoke on the planet. I didn't know this kind of thing— *Is that Patti LuPone?!*"

Let me explain: To the rest of the world, Julia Roberts is a big star. But I am a drama geek. To me, seeing the original *Evita* in the flesh outshone seeing every movie star on the planet. I was closer than the front row. I was practically onstage. And I was hearing my total Broadway idol sing the song that made her famous, "Don't Cry For Me, Argentina." It gave me chills. I mean, my feet left the floor and I floated around the room when I heard her sing. It was just amazing. When the last of her notes faded, the room was totally silent for a full ten seconds, then exploded into cheers and stomping. I just stood there, my jaw practically on the floor.

The next few hours flew by as big stars traded with wet-behind-the-ears stage rookies, singing the greatest songs ever sung on Broadway. By the time we stumbled out of there, it was the middle of the night, the limo driver was asleep behind the wheel of our car, and Fritz looked like he'd been running a marathon. But I was still walking on air.

"Ohmigod, could you believe how great that girl's voice was?" I gushed. "Ohmigod. It was like I never heard anyone sing 'I Don't Know How to Love Him' before in my life. It sounded like a whole new song. Did you see Malaika? Could you believe she was

89

there? Why didn't she sing? I wish she sang; she's got a beautiful voice. I'll bet she—"

He shut my mouth with a kiss—a real one, the kind that makes you feel like your lips are on fire and the only thing that can put it out is . . . Let's just say it was a great kiss. I loved how my tottering heels made me tall enough to reach Jeb without straining. After a few moments he even stepped down off the curb and stood on the street while our lips continued to tickle each other. I rested my elbows on his shoulders and enjoyed the different kiss angle—face-to-face—and finally just had to throw my arms around his neck and give him a warm, close hug.

I felt like I was falling. I was definitely falling. It wasn't just the kisses making me dizzy—it was vertigo, from looking down from cloud nine.

"I should take you home," he murmured.

"No, I don't want this night to end," I complained. "Can't we go to the China Club? It's right down the street, and I've always wanted to go. . . ."

"Oh, I dunno," Jeb moaned. "It can get kind of crazy in there."

"Pleeease?"

He rolled his eyes. "Okay, fine," he said. "It's late on a Monday; how crowded can it be?"

Answer: pretty darn crowded. Packed, in fact. Moving through the main floor was like being in a sardine can decorated by Dolce & Gabbana. It was wild, though. Disco lights flickered everywhere: stars were projected on the walls; the walls pulsed with various shades of purple and blue. And over the mahogany bar, wavy hunks of wood studded with lights created a funky canopy. The music was a mash-up of familiar tunes as mixed by a deejay.

A velvet rope separated the tables from the dance floor. Of course, for Jeb the velvet rope was pulled aside, but he shook his head, grabbed my hand, and pulled me through the sea of sweaty bodies up to the VIP roof deck of the club.

Up here it was slightly less crowded. But as I looked back, I realized Fritz hadn't made it through the half-naked crowd.

"We lost Fritz!" I shouted, and Jeb laughed.

"About time," he answered me.

We took a stroll around the terrace, then entered the Shei Shei Lounge, which looked out from the sec-ond floor down onto the street. This was even more VIP-ey, which meant we had enough air to breathe and even found a corner of one of the lush maroon couches to sit on.

"I have to go to the ladies' room," I shouted into Jeb's ear.

He nodded. "Over there," he said, and I stood and worked my way over to the corner he'd indicated.

Once I made it inside, I checked my lipstick in the huge gilt mirror and then picked a stall. Almost im-mediately a gaggle of drunk girls came stumbling in.

"Did you see him?" One giggled.

"Jeb Razor? Sh—yeah," another said.

"He's so hot!"

I smiled to myself. Indeed, he was hot—and he was with me. Their voices were like popcorn hopping around in the air over their heads. Then the smile froze on my face.

91

"I heard he was making out with that girl from the Calvin Klein billboard."

"Who? The blond one?"

"I don't know; I think so."

"That was the other guy from his band, the one who was a Mouseketeer."

"No, not him; he's in rehab."

"I'd make out with him."

"Ew! In rehab?"

"No, I mean Jeb. Do you think I've got a shot?"

"Go talk to him. Remember last week, when you ended up in the bathroom with Joey Fatone?"

"No! I did?"

"You're such a slut!"

They exploded in laughter (popcorn everywhere!) and tottered back out of the bathroom, their lipstick fixed. I just sat there. How could I have been so stupid? Jeb couldn't be my boyfriend. He wasn't with me. He was a celebrity. He belonged here, where gaggles of girls would line up to give him whatever he wanted in the bathroom of a club.

I stepped out of the stall and looked at myself in the mirror. My curly brown hair sprung out from my head like a mass of octopus legs. My skin was pale white, almost translucent, making my thick lips look like stupid pink bubblegum worms. Who did I think I was? Not a Broadway star—just a girl who got a lucky break. Not a TV star—just another reality-show flash in the pan. And most certainly not the little blond girl from the Calvin Klein billboard.

I stepped out of the bathroom and saw exactly what I expected. Jeb was still at his spot on the

92

couch, but he was surrounded by women. Thin, willowy women with blond hair pulled into ponytails on the tops of their heads, half clothed in expensively trashy ensembles, their skin evenly tanned to a pricey-looking orange hue. They looked like a troop of aliens from Planet Steal-your-boyfriend. And they were all over Jeb.

And Jeb . . . he didn't look unhappy about it.

I watched him, being his same charming self with those girls as he was with me. Chatting, laughing—didn't he see how fake they were? How could he even enjoy their company? They were gross. He was gross. He was so gross, the way he smiled at them, it reminded me of someone. It was exactly like . . .

Ugh. It was exactly the way Joey used to talk to other girls. And then I'd be all "Who were you talking to?" and he'd be all "You're paranoid" and then I'd find out he was cheating on me yet again.

Blech.

Ugh!

I suddenly felt very, very claustrophobic. I heard a rushing noise in my ears and my vision dimmed a little, almost like I was going to pass out or barf. There were too many people around me. I felt like I couldn't breathe. I didn't want to walk back to Jeb and see him give me the same fake smile he was giving everyone else. Correction: I couldn't walk back to Jeb. I had to get out of there.

Now.

Now!

I turned right and made a beeline for the carpeted stairs, clunking down them in my stupid tall stilettos.

I tried to keep my face from crumpling into some kind of embarrassing crying thing, but I could feel tears itching at the corners of my eyes. I just felt so sick! And so grossed out! I had to . . .

The door! I saw the door across the crowded dance floor and shoved my way across, sending clutch bags flying and leaving at least two toes with stiletto holes in them. As I passed through the door I was flooded with relief: That was a close call. I'd definitely been falling, but caught myself just in time.

The clear white moon seemed to mirror the revelation I'd just been given. Jeb was nothing but a distraction from what was really important—being great in this show so I could have a career. If I let him reach into my chest and grab my heart, and then started running around trying to get it back from him, I'd suck onstage and end up back in Hamilton, New Jersey, doing community theater with the local Lunchbox Players. It was bad enough he'd kept me out so late; I had rehearsal in the morning, and three hours of sleep was going to show. Jeb wasn't Prince Charming. He was nothing but Joey with fancier facial hair.

The cobwebs cleared out of my mind, the rushing gone from my ears, my vision clear, I walked the three blocks down to my apartment building. I didn't hear the limo sidle up behind me, and Jeb didn't appear, calling out the window for me. I was all alone, and that was fine with me. I was here to do a job, not to have some kind of fairy-tale romance.

No matter how amazing it felt.

Chapter Six

"All right, people. Are we ready?"

I stood just outside the door of the theater, in the lobby, listening as Seth rounded everyone up. I felt like a pile of laundry. I had made it home by three A.M., but once my head hit the pillow I was wide-awake, my mind running a million miles an hour with competing images of the wonderful night I'd had versus the sight of Jeb acting just like Joey. It was enough to give a girl insomnia. Not to mention the fact that Tina heard me come in, and came in all excited to hear about my adventures. I was so overwrought—all the excitement, all the wonderful feelings of being with him, and then the crushing letdown when I realized who (and what) he really was—that of course I dissolved into tears. She sat there gazing at me with her gray eyes like two deep rainclouds, patting my shoulder and trying to shush me, and finally taking my head into her lap like I do with my little sisters, and smoothing the curls against my head. I remembered feeling this way with my mom, barely, when I was so young that I only had three younger siblings—it felt natural, and I let her soothe me into a troubled slumber.

"So complicated," I heard her say as I drifted off. "Too difficult. Too much trouble, too much pain in your little heart." I didn't notice when she left, but it felt like five seconds later when my alarm went off. The sun had risen and it was time to get back up, but I'd barely had two hours of sleep. So the bags under my eyes were carrying their own travel valises.

The main thing I'd resolved in my sleepless night was to stay away from Jeb. To that end, I had to avoid being at rehearsal early—major chat time—and would have to find some reason to cut out afterward. The rest of the time—that is, during the rare breaks Seth was required by law to allow during our grueling rehearsal sessions—I would have to just keep working as hard as I could, throwing myself into total commitment to craft. I'd become a dancing-singing-acting machine, like some unholy amalgam of C-3PO and Ann Reinking.

Okay, so maybe it seemed a little extreme. And I highly doubt that Ann Reinking, the Broadway legend, former paramour of Bob Fosse, and star of the movie *All That Jazz*, ever stood trembling in a theater lobby waiting until the last possible second to enter a rehearsal out of abject terror of seeing her leading man—not to mention being whacked out on zero sleep and guiltily avoiding the curious gaze of a camera lens held by an equally exhausted cameraman. But this was the only way I had to salvage my chance at stardom.

When it sounded like Seth was ready to take a riding crop to the rest of the cast, I clanged open the door and came running in like I'd been running since Ninth Avenue. "Sorry, sorry," I said. "Sorry I'm late."

"You're not quite late," Seth grumbled. "But don't cut it so close. I like everyone warmed up before we start."

I ducked my head in acknowledgment and took a new spot on the stage, all the way downstage, near the audience, and as far as possible from Jeb. Out of the corner of my eye I could see him leaning toward me, making "psst" noises and trying to get my attention.

I don't think anyone has ever concentrated quite so hard on her morning stretches. You'd have thought I was doing brain surgery from how focused I was on my hamstrings.

That morning we worked on the scene in which Jeb's character, Daniel, and my character, Tinka, break up. I mean, you couldn't write a more ironic situation, could you? I'd been having trouble with this one—spitting out hateful words at him, then singing them, then dancing in opposition to his moves, in a furious pas-de-drama. But today it all just clicked. I acted, sang, and danced the hell out of that piece. At one point Tinka sings a line that says, "Why don't you join a boy band and be pretty with the other sellouts?" Let's just say I delivered it with a vehemence I'd never been able to harness before.

Seth ran me through it three times, and couldn't find anything to complain about. That's how good I was.

97

And by the end of the third run-through of the number, Jeb had stopped trying to get my attention, and seemed to get the message that I'd left him the night before for a reason. I had to give him credit: He had enough class to realize I was on to his game and not try to give me some cheesy explanation. I wasn't interested. I wasn't giving him an in. Never mind the disappointment in his eyes—I'd hardened my heart to any possibility between us. And true to form, when we broke for lunch I saw him turn away from me and start flirting with that little monkey-looking Paula girl.

Guys are dogs. Woof.

I thought about taking a nap in the seats of the theater, like some of the other cast members did sometimes, curling themselves around so their heads were in one seat, their knees were in the next, and their butts stuck out around the armrest, but I'd downed my breakfast coffees without the usual banana to soak up the acid, and my stomach was really unhappy with me. So I plodded out to the street and got a four-dollar beef-and-kimchi roll from the Korean takeout place down the street.

On my way back I paused in the doorway to the theater, trying to open the stubborn top of my ginseng-packed vitamin water. (It's a serious Catch-22 when you don't have the energy to get to your energy juice, don't you think?) I swear I wasn't hiding there on purpose, but when I heard Seth and his assistant, Donna, enter the lobby for a private pow-wow, I wasn't exactly motivated to leave, either.

"Oh, she's on fire," Seth said.

"I know, she's really improved," Donna agreed.

"I don't know how she did it. Claire was Ebola in character shoes when we started rehearsals, and suddenly she's a goddamned Broadway baby. I'm amazed."

"So are you open to the possibility that this new cast might not be a total disaster?" Donna teased him.

"Maybe—knock on wood—maybe it'll be halfway decent," Seth reluctantly admitted.

"And you'll be less hard on her, right?"

"Let's not get carried away. I have to keep her on her toes." That made me smile. So I was doing all right. If that was the case, I could take any criticism he was dishing out. I wanted to get even better, and he did know what he was talking about.

"I don't know what you guys are so happy about," a third voice chimed in. It took a moment to place it. Then I realized it was Mary-Ellen Murray, the executive producer of *Unscripted*. "I was counting on her stinking up the place to make the show a hit. It's doing all right, but all this nice-nice crap is going to start being really boring, really soon. How am I going to get the ratings during sweeps week if everything's all happy and nice?"

"I don't know, but don't screw things up for me," Seth snapped. "I had to let you people stick an amateur into my show so you'd help me with financing. If it turns out she's halfway decent, that's just too bad for you."

"Hmph." Wow, Seth had silenced Mary-Ellen Murray, the most intimidating woman ever to wear a Donna Karan suit. I had to hand it to him.

Then the full meaning of what she had said sank in, and I looked up at Fritz with an expression so annoyed and shocked, I saw his face twist into a grin of amusement. I managed to keep silent as they continued on their merry way to the administrative office of the theater, and then I let out a tremendous "Ugh!"

I thought of Fiona and how she and I had been manipulated by the first season of this reality show, back at Hamilton High. The show's director would stop at nothing to get the ratings, even if it meant totally humiliating our friend Pete—and possibly putting him in harm's way. Now it was happening again. Mary-Ellen wanted a flop, and I was being difficult by not giving it to her. Welcome to reality television, where pain and suffering translate into huge cash payouts for everyone except the person suffering the pain. I felt my old familiar friend, fury, well up in my gut. My jaw closed, then set in a teeth-clenching grimace.

"Hey, Mary-Ellen," I said into Fritz's lens. "Too bad for you, I don't suck as badly as you think. Hope you get your ratings anyway."

Fritz's grin faded, and he hit the stop button on his camera and lowered it to look seriously at me.

"I'm going to tape over that," he said.

"No, don't," I insisted.

"Claire, it's not smart. You shouldn't let her know that you overheard her, and you definitely can't razz her like that. She's going to see it for sure."

"Good! I want her to," I snapped.

"No, you really—"

"Yeah, I really do! Fritz, you don't understand. I've got what it takes to make this show great. I'm going to listen to every word Seth says from now on, and he's going to love me. So I don't need this stupid show. If she fires me, that's fine—I'll be so good, he'll want to keep me anyway. I want to be a Broadway actress, not a TV star. I'm not going to give her the flop she wants."

"I'm not saying you have to give her what she wants. Be great onstage, but don't burn your bridges with *Unscripted*," he said. But I was angry, and his tiny ice cubes of sensible words were no match for the flaming fury in my head.

"You just hand that tape over to them," I told him. "If she's not meant to see it, then she won't. I'll take my chances. And if I find out you didn't deliver it, I'll tell her myself."

Fritz shrugged, then brought the camera back up to his face and switched it back on. I went back inside to chow down with Malaika, then finish the afternoon's rehearsal. I'd made my statement. Now I wanted to get back to work, period.

Did I say period? As I dragged myself home that night I felt more like a colon. As in, I felt like ass. I cracked myself up thinking that one up, let me tell you. It's amazing what no sleep, not enough food, and too much singing, stretching, and emoting can do to a girl. I was practically hysterical when I got to my building.

"Hey! What's so funny?" a voice said. I turned and saw Jonah riding up on his skateboard. When he got to me he stepped off it and kind of kicked it up into his hands, then stood there looking like he didn't really know what to say next.

"Hey." I laughed. I was genuinely glad to see him. "Nothing. I mean, I was just making myself laugh, but really I'm delirious from working too hard. Are you here to pick up Tina?"

"Um, no," he said. Now he looked really uncomfortable. "She doesn't know I'm here," he admitted. "I mean, she hasn't been taking my calls. She won't call me or e-mail me or anything. I sent her a letter and she had it sent back to me. I'm kind of at a loss."

"Oh." I had no idea what to say. I looked around me. Fritz had told me he was packing up and going home early—my late night had seriously taken it out of him, and he joked that he wasn't as young and resilient as me—and I didn't see a replacement, so I took Jonah by the arm and pulled him out of the foot traffic going in and out of my building so we could talk.

"I heard your phone messages," I admitted. "I don't know what her deal is. I told her to call you back, and I think she wants to, but she's really hung up on this idea that she doesn't want any complications," I said.

"I don't want to give her complications!" he insisted earnestly. "I want to make her life easier. I can help her if she'd just let me in. She needs someone to take care of her, Claire. She's been taking care of herself since she was a kid. All I want to do is take some of the burden off her—and be the guy she can depend on."

As opposed to my dad. That was the unspoken truth, of course. My dad was the guy she couldn't depend on, and Jonah was paying the price for that. I wanted to make up for the injustice of it all. I wanted to help make it right.

I could see how deeply Jonah felt for my sister. It was all right there in his eyes: This boy was in serious pain. I thought back to how Jeb and Joey had both fooled me, and burned with anger at my dad. And it all made me wonder how Tina could let the one good guy on the planet get away from her.

"I'll talk to her again," I said lamely. "I know that sounds stupid. I can't make her act right. Just try to be patient, okay? You're a really good guy, Jonah. I'm sure she'll see the light one of these days."

"I dunno." He studied his sneakers, looking almost like a little boy, with his hair all messy and his face so sad. He reminded me of my baby brother when his remote-control car got run over. I couldn't help but give him a long, warm, sisterly hug.

"Hang in there," I said. "Try to take care of yourself in the meantime, huh?"

"I guess," he mumbled. "Thanks anyway."

"I know how you feel, if that makes it any better." I sighed.

"That sucks for you."

We both kind of laughed, and then I stepped back, feeling a little awkward. I gave his arm a squeeze.

"I'd tell you to come upstairs, but I'm not sure that would—"

"Nah, nah," he said, his face flushing. He dropped his skateboard back down on the ground and rolled

103

it back and forth a few times. "I appreciate your talking to me. My friends all think I'm totally whipped, but Tina's really worth it," he said. "It's good to talk to someone who understands the whole thing."

"I understand, but I wish I could help."

"You did." He gave me that goofy grin, and the sadness seemed to retreat a little. "I'm okay! Just see, you know, what you can do."

"I will!" I promised, and waved as he clattered away down the sidewalk, narrowly missing an old couple before he hopped the curb into the street.

"Sorry!" he called back to them, then yelled, "Thanks, Claire!" to me, and then he was gone. I smiled at the old couple, who rolled their eyes as if to say, "What is with you stupid young people?" I shrugged—*I don't know what's with us, but I agree, we really are stupid,* I thought, and then went upstairs to my apartment.

Once inside, I turned on the TV and collapsed onto the couch, and was snoring before the first commercial break. I barely woke up when Tina shook me and walked me, half dreaming, to my bedroom. I had less than a week before my opening night, and I was working myself at a punishing pace. Were my words to Fritz grounded in any kind of fact? Did I really have what it took to make it in this show? What if I didn't? Then Mary-Ellen would really get her disaster.

I had to be right. I just had to. Because as of this morning, I'd given up everything so I could go after this goal. And I couldn't let anything stop me. Not heartbreak. Not hard work. And not self-doubt.

Especially not self-doubt!

Chapter Seven

I was standing behind the curtain, staring at the thick fabric, smelling the heady mix of dust, wood, resin, makeup, and sweat that could be bottled and sold under the name "Opening Night." I don't know who'd buy it—bulimics who need incentive to barf? Flat-lining heart-attack victims who need a jolt? Ex-Mormons craving excitement?

Then it was go time. The curtain whooshed up in a rush and I faced an audience full of expectant faces, peering up at me through the gloom. Applause rippled through the room, then gradually receded in a decrescendo that sounded like the end of a rainstorm. I opened my mouth, and realized I had no idea what was supposed to come out.

I looked down. I wasn't wearing my *Twentynothings* costume. I was in Renaissance dress. I realized with a shock that I had missed several rehearsals, and the play had been completely rewritten before opening night. All my cocky self-assuredness had brought me here, in front of this crowd, with nothing to say. I was totally lost.

I swallowed as an overheated rash of humiliation spread from my heart and radiated out my arms, to my feet, and up my throat to make my face burn bright red. I could hear people shifting uncomfortably in their seats. There was a cough. Then another one. Then silence. And I stood there, not knowing what to say, unable to run off the stage, but naked and exposed in the glare of the spotlight.

Urr! Urr! Urr! Urr! Urr! Urr! Urr! Urr!

I sat bolt upright in bed. I'd never in my life been so grateful to hear the sound of my clock-radio's obnoxious alarm. As my thumping heart slowly returned to normal, I felt relief flooding through my veins, though a part of me couldn't quite believe the dream wasn't real.

"Are you okay?" Tina asked. She was standing in the doorway in her Nick and Nora tank-top jammies, looking like a college kid instead of the high-powered lawyer she really is. "You look like you just saw Rosie O'Donnell in a thong."

"Worse," I said. "I just had this awful dream. I was onstage and it was opening night, but I had the wrong costume on, and I didn't know any of my lines."

"That's the actor's nightmare!" she cheered, coming into my room—I was grateful to see she had two mugs of coffee, and took mine so she could sit on my bed.

"It's a thing? There's an industry-wide nightmare?"

"Sure! Didn't you ever hear of it? True actors always have that dream. So does anyone who's got performance anxiety, I guess, but mostly actors. So that's a good sign! You're really ready for opening night!"

My relief gave way to an oogy sense of foreboding. "It's tonight." I groaned. "I don't know if I can do it."

"You survived the nightmare, right?" Tina tucked her feet under her and sipped her inky black java.

"Barely."

"You're going to be great."

I gave her a wan smile. "If you say so. Hey, will you help me sue Seth if I suck?"

"Very funny." Tina sat back against the wall and squeezed my calf. "I don't think I'd have time anyway. This case is kicking my butt, and the partner in charge of it is pawning all his work off on me so he can take his family on vacation in the Hamptons."

"I know! I've barely seen you all week!" I complained. "I thought we were supposed to be roommates."

"I'm sorry. I didn't realize how much time this dumb case was going to take."

"What about that other thing?" I asked. "The courtroom case. The judge and everything."

"I'm not thinking about it," Tina admitted, glowering into the depths of her mug. "I'm going to have to talk to my boss the minute he gets back. I'll lay it on the line. I've gotten everything so ready and done so much research and put it into such an organized form, he's got everything he needs to walk into the courtroom himself and win that case with the jury. I'm sure he'll give up once he sees how easy I've made it for him."

"Why don't you just do it?" I wanted to know. "You've done all that work; you must know the facts cold."

"Cut it out; you'll give me my own actor's nightmare." She scooted off the bed. "Anyway, it's back to the old grind. Do you mind if I hit the shower first?"

"Go ahead. I don't even think I'm going to bother," I called after her, realizing with a thud in my chest that I'd forgotten to mention my conversation with Jonah to her. Like she'd said, we'd barely seen each other, and I still felt a little shy with her. I didn't know how to broach such a sensitive subject.

"Ugh, no shower?" I heard the water go on.

"I've got rehearsal all day," I called out. "I'll just have to take another one before showtime anyway."

"Suit yourself," she said, and the bathroom door closed, which sealed off any more conversation for the moment.

I got up and pulled on my sweats and a sports bra. The butterflies in my stomach were waltzing around in three-four time, and I knew they'd be doing the tango before long. I went out to the kitchen and scrambled some eggs for me and Tina. The toast was popping up out of the toaster as she came in, hair blow-dried straight and pulled back into a ponytail. Her red power suit looked like armor: She was a different person.

"Thanks!" she said as she poured herself a new

mug of coffee and sipped it, this time looking less like a college kid and more like she was about to question the coffee regarding its whereabouts on the night of a murder. "Aren't you going to eat?"

I gazed down at the fluffy eggs on my plate, next to a hopeful pool of ketchup, and grimaced. "I'm trying," I said. "I'm nervous."

"Come on, you have to eat."

The air in the kitchen was pierced by the electric trilling of our phone. "That's got to be Dennis," Tina said. "I'd better get it, or he'll call my cell phone next." She picked up the phone, and I poked my fork into my eggs, trying to will myself to stick some in my mouth. I was so sure I was going to gag. But my stomach rumbled with hunger.

"What? No, I can't. . . . I mean, of course I understand, but I really think . . ." Tina's end of her conversation didn't sound like it was going so great. I eyeballed her, and saw the color draining from her face until she was as pale as Gene Simmons in the first half of his KISS makeup. "Dennis, I've never . . . I appreciate that. Yes, I know, but I was just thinking a better strategy might be to . . . um. Oh. Yes." She paused, took a deep, shaky breath, and nodded. "Fine. I'll call you afterward."

"Rosie O'Donnell has to stop walking around in that thong," I said to her, making a joke about the devastated expression on her face. "Sorry. Is something wrong?"

"There's a deposition today. Dennis was supposed to come back to depose this witness, and he can't do it. So I have to."

"Oh."

"Yeah."

"Tina, I'm sure you know how to do it."

"I do know how. But I hate it. There's going to be people there watching, and it's all going to get recorded by the court reporter, and I hate this crap."

"Have you done it before?"

"Yes, but I almost passed out."

"Okay. Listen." I stood up and took her hands in mine. "Look at me. Now, breathe in deeply. Right? Now out. You're not going to pass out." I led her through one of the breathing exercises I'd learned at drama camp, which was developed to rid actors of distraction so they could concentrate on their work. I felt her hands stop trembling and saw that vein in her neck thud a little slower as she did the exercise.

"Okay," she said. "I'll do that later. I feel better."

"No, you don't," I admitted. "But at least you're not going to jump out of your skin."

"I do. I feel better." She tried to smile, but it came out kind of crooked. She sat in front of her plate of eggs and wrinkled her nose.

Neither one of us felt much like eating.

Fritz came in the front door, silently pointing the camera in our direction. We glared at him, then looked at each other and laughed.

"Okay, good luck," she said, abandoning her eggs to the fridge. "I mean, break a leg."

"You too," I said, sliding my plate next to hers. "I mean, good luck."

We hugged, me reaching up on my tiptoes to match her height in her executive-style pumps. I felt

110

her arms tighten around me fiercely, as if she were trying to take strength from me and fill me with it at the same time. I hugged back, willing her to feel as thrilled with performing as I did.

"I'll see you tonight," she said, turning her back on Fritz and grabbing her briefcase on her way out the door.

"Okay," I called after her. Then I turned to Fritz. "You want some eggs?" I asked.

Thank goodness, after that first nerve-racking day, Jeb hadn't tried to rekindle our fake friendship. So I didn't have to show up at rehearsal almost late, and I could spend some extra minutes warming up and doing vocal exercises. I was going to need all the warm-ups I could get. In the past week I'd kept the edge I gained when I cut Jeb out of my life, but I wasn't sure if I'd improved enough to really look good on opening night. I didn't want to just be good-considering-she's-only-some-kid-from-reality-TV. I wanted to shock everyone with my honest talent and hard work. And I didn't have the sure feeling that I was there yet.

As we did our group warm-up, I saw Paula sidle up to Jeb and lean into him, giving him a lascivious little wink as she moved her body in a flirty, look-at-my-boobs fashion. His face didn't show any surprise, though he didn't flirt back, either. He just took it in, like the celebrity ego-monster he was. I thought it was gross, the way Paula was flaunting their relationship (or whatever it was). And I also felt a knife-slice of jealousy cut through my heart as I tried not to watch. I guess there was a part of me that had hoped to be wrong, and expected things to work out between us. But they wouldn't. And that was fine. I'd channel the pain into my performance, that was all.

But Paula was all over Jeb all day. That was a lot of channeling. I tried to use the distracting fact that she was practically writhing around him like an anaconda stalking a tasty-looking monkey. Every time I saw them hanging out together, I forced myself to focus harder on the show. By the end of the six-hour rehearsal, I was focusing so hard I thought my brain was going to leak out my ears. Sheesh. Some people should get a room. In hell.

Malaika sat me down between rehearsal and our performance and forced me to eat some dumplings at Ollie's. I was hungry enough that I got them down, and to my relief they stayed there.

"You've been on Broadway before," I said to her.

"Yeah, I was a chorus girl in *42nd Street*," she said.

"And you survived?"

"Apparently." She shrugged. "Hey. Listen. It's just like any other opening night."

I made a "phhht" sound. "Sure, only bigger, with more people, who paid sixty-five dollars a ticket, and *The New York Times*, and cameras, with a million people just waiting for me to screw up."

"Right." She grinned. "Just like any other opening night."

She finally got me to laugh.

We went up to the roof of my building and gazed out at the city for a while, just having a little quiet time. I hoped it was at least picturesque enough for Fritz, who looked bored out of his mind. I was just trying to keep myself sane long enough to get on-stage and do my job. Across the river, I could see the long, low cliffs of New Jersey, with the high-rise condos of Weehawken, Hoboken, and a town that actually called itself West New York. It was just a hop across the water, but I felt like I was a Grand Canyon away from the shrieking, overwrought, hysterical little girl who'd ruled her high school theater productions and thought she knew everything. Had that really been me? And now that I'd left that past behind, what lay in my future?

Before too long we were crowded into our dressing rooms at the theater and putting on our makeup, with help from the amazing Enid. I had seen her around the theater, as squat and gray and unglamorous as anybody's grandma, and thought she was the head usher. It turned out she was a one-woman cosmetics cavalcade, attacking our faces with a level of old-school skill and artistry which made her famous in every theater. Apparently, we were supposed to learn how to do this ourselves at some point, but Enid was here to make sure we got it right, and she was such a perfectionist, she just ended up doing it herself.

"Let me do your . . . You have to . . . All right. Put on the mascara yourself," Enid barked at me. "Jesus, you're going to put an eye out if you quiver like that."

"I'm nervous," I complained.

"So be nervous. All the more reason you need some help in the complexion department."

"All right, all right."

The theater we were in was an old restored beauty. The owners had added some conveniences, like a few more bathrooms for the audience, but there was no denying it was an old building. Which I liked. It felt like generations of nervous actresses had slicked on their mascara in this small room, with its huge mirror lined with clear lightbulbs and one small filthy window looking out onto an air shaft. The very paint on the walls seemed like it was saturated with leftover nervous sweat. How many bouquets of roses had filled this room over the years? I wondered. How many people had studied themselves in this mirror? My own roses—from my parents—as well as a riot of daffodils from Fiona, Pete, and Baxter—took up all the available space. There was even a box of chocolates from Joey. I finished my mascara and sighed. There was nothing to do now but wait.

Enid left, and almost immediately there was another knock on the door. I was retying the laces of the Doc Martens that were part of my costume, and I thought she had just forgotten something, so I shouted, "Come in!"

In walked Jeb. I broke the lace on my boot.

"Crap," I hissed.

"Sorry," he said.

"No problem. I have, like, five extra everythings. I even have extra fishnets ripped in the exact right places," I blabbered nervously. "I always like to be overprepared."

"I know." He watched me start to relace my boot.

114

I was just glad I had something to do with my hands. "Are you okay?" he asked.

"Sure, yes," I said politely.

"Well, I just wanted to say I know you'll do great tonight," he said.

"Oh." I looked up at him. "Thank you," I said.

"I mean it. You've been really brave. You walked in here with everything set against you, and you've worked incredibly hard. I really admire you. You're going to be great tonight, but no matter what happens, I think you're a star."

He stood there, and I felt like a giant awkward mess. I didn't even know where to look. Was he being for real? He sounded for real. This was so nice. Yet I knew that he was a dog. I was totally confused.

"Thanks," I said finally, emotions roiling in my head. "I know you're going to do great, too."

He kept standing there. He looked really unsure, like he wanted to say something else, but couldn't figure out how. He nodded, swallowed, shifted his weight a few times. But whatever it was, it wasn't coming out.

"Thank you for setting up those extra sessions for me," I added. "With your trainers. That really helped me."

A cloud passed over his face and he nodded. Whatever he'd been about to say, I guess he changed his mind about.

"No problem," he said quickly. "So have a good show." He shuffled out the door like he couldn't wait to escape, and I felt relieved to see him go.

"You too," I said, and heard the door click closed.

I mean, nice is nice, and encouragement is great, but he was just making me more nervous. "Better go smooch with Paula before we have to go on," I muttered to myself, trying to force myself to remember that I didn't like him anymore. Not like that. Because my heart was pounding, crush-style, in total opposition to what my head was telling it.

This was all getting horribly confusing.

"Places, everybody!" the stage manager shouted, adjusting his headset as he raced around to all our dressing rooms. "Places for the opening! Break a leg!"

And then there I was, standing behind the same heavy curtain from my dream. Only this time I was in the right costume (yes, I checked). All of us were ranged across the stage, a tiny glow-tape X marking each of our spots. Our eyes brushed one another's in the dim light, and I felt a swell of affection that had nothing to do with how I felt about each of these people individually, and everything to do with what we were about to do. We were soldiers who were about to fight a battle, partners in a project that only we could understand.

It wasn't just affection. I loved everyone on that stage at that moment. Paula wasn't Paula; she was Dannica, the upbeat Midwestern girl who follows her guy to the big city only to have her dreams dashed, and discover that she's got more inner life than she'd ever imagined. Malaika didn't even stand like herself; she'd taken on the twin personalities of Kelvin—not the dichotomy of man/woman, but the split between the carefree spirit he showed the world as a drag queen and the deeper, more soulful side that Steve fell in love with, against his own will. Jeb smoothed his hands over Daniel's Armani suit. And I found that I wasn't Claire. I was Tinka, the girl with big dreams and a tiny bank account, looking for a community in the abandoned buildings of the Lower East Side.

We were going to do this. Together. No matter what else was going on. Music swelled, and I heard a whoosh.

Curtain up.

I really couldn't tell you what happened between eight and eleven P.M. that night. I know it went past: I've seen the tapes and I know I was there. But in my mind it was nothing but a blur. It's like I was taken over by some kind of muse, as corny as that must sound. From the moment we began singing the sad, thrilling opening song, all of our voices joining together to tell the story of our friendship, I felt like some kind of outside energy took me over, taking the steps I'd learned in countless rehearsals and making them completely new for the audience watching them. It was like there were two of me, one making sure I got everything right, and one that didn't care, but just wanted to be inside the character of Tinka, weeping at her pain and celebrating her happiness. And like there was none of me—just a speck that got sucked up into the giant wonderful machine of the theater.

Maybe if you're not an actor, you don't know what I'm talking about. Or maybe you do—maybe everyone feels this way when they get to do what they're

117

meant to do. I'm just saying, the show went great. And at the end, when we returned to our opening song and retold the story from beginning to end in the space of five passionate, tear-jerking minutes, then joined hands to bow, the audience told us we'd been right as they exploded into wild applause and whooping appreciation. Tinka vanished and I cracked a wide, happy grin that was a hundred percent Claire as I looked back out at them, savoring every second of their attention and love.

In other words, the show was a hit. And I didn't suck.

We ran offstage after a bunch of curtain calls and hugged each other. I even hugged Fritz, messing up his camera angle as I came at him in a rush. Enid helped me out of my costume and showed me how to slather my face in cold cream to take as much of that crap off as I could, and patted me on the shoulder.

"You wasn't half-bad, sweetheart," she told me, which I knew was high praise.

"Come on, we're heading for Sardi's," Seth ordered. Sardi's is this restaurant in the Theater District where everyone goes after a show to wait for the reviews. Ugh! The walls are lined with caricature drawings of every great star ever to walk the boards of Broadway. I'd driven past it and imagined heading in there to celebrate my opening night, and now I really would.

By the time I got there with the rest of the cast, the place was packed. I found Tina in the back, near the rest rooms, looking like she'd rather be anywhere

118

but in this crush of people. I grabbed her hand grate-fully.

"Who are all these people?" she asked.

"I have no idea," I told her. "My parents are over there. Will you come over and—"

"Sure," she said, her gray eyes widening in terror.

"Glass of champagne first?"

"Sure." She downed it and accompanied me across the room, where the four of us tried to chat. But everyone was uncomfortable. My dad couldn't really look at Tina. My mom was gracious, trying to chat with her about anything and everything, but it was hard for her, too: She's a good Catholic mom, and the all-too-human evidence of her husband's premarriage peccadilloes freaked her out. And, of course, we were right next to the table where Jeb and Paula were entertaining a couple of the guys from his band, their model/actress girlfriends, and a bevy of reporters from every tabloid in the universe. Paula was draped over Jeb's shoulders like a skinny blond mink stole.

Tina followed my gaze as I kept looking over at them. She nudged me. "If it bothers you, why are you letting it happen?" she asked.

"I don't need more complications," I answered, and she nodded. If anyone understood a statement like that, it was her. But she looked kind of sad when I said it, too. We'd finally found some solid common ground, and it wasn't making either of us particularly happy. But at least we were calm, and getting our work done . . . right?

Before too long I was finished with the dumb party.

119

My adrenaline ran out. The show was the best part of the night; this was just uncomfortable and annoying. All I wanted to do was go home and replay the whole performance in my head, savoring the good parts and planning how to improve anything I could. I think my parents were relieved when I pointed out they had a long drive home. I walked them to the parking lot and waited while their car was brought out. Dad grumbled about the expense and I kissed him on the cheek, then hugged my mom and sent them on their way. And then Tina and I plodded home, arm in arm.

"You were amazing," she told me. "Better than amazing. You were magnetic. It was like you owned the stage. . . . I was so nervous for you until I saw how comfortable you were up there, as if you were born to be a star. I knew you could do it."

"Thank you. Oh God, it felt so good," I admitted. "Now I just have to do it again. And again and again and again . . ."

We laughed and went up to the apartment, where the answering machine was blinking spastically.

"Claire, it's Fee," Fiona cheered. "I hope your show went really great! We'll see you soon; we've got our tickets! I wanted to see what you thought of *Unscripted*, though. I can't believe that crap!"

Beep.

"Ohmigod, Claire, it's Pete, I'll bet you're a star! So are you going to sue *Unscripted*? Those bastards, they'll stop at nothing!"

Beep.

"Tina, it's Jonah; will you call me when you get this? Before you watch the show?"

Beep.

What the . . .

"Should we watch it?" Tina asked.

"I don't know. Do you want to call Jonah?"

"Oh, I can't handle a conversation," she groaned. "Let's just call it up on TiVo and have a look."

We turned on the video recorder and called up that night's episode of *Unscripted*. The episodes had been piling up on the TiVo hard drive since the first one. I meant to watch them, but between regular rehearsals and my extra sessions, I just didn't have the time or energy. And of course, I didn't have the heart to watch my beautiful date on tape—since I knew how it really ended. Can you imagine literally being able to replay your biggest heartache? I had no idea what everyone was so hysterical about. All I had been doing since last week was working—what could they have found to make a fuss about?

I watched uncomfortably as I ran through my paces at a bunch of rehearsals. There I was, standing outside the theater, waiting till I knew I wouldn't have to talk to Jeb when I walked in (though they deleted my little speech to Mary-Ellen later in the day). There were interviews with some of the other cast members.

"I don't know what's going on with them," Malaika said. "I just know Claire's working really hard, and it shows."

"Did they have a thing?" Paula simpered. "I had no idea. Well, it's over now, I'll tell you that."

Then they switched to footage of Jeb and Paula out on the town, dancing at a huge club, bigger than the China Club. They didn't go to Broadway karaoke night at the Supper Club, but they partied like rock stars. Which is what he was, so it made sense. It made me feel really gross, though.

"We can turn this off," Tina offered.

"No, it's fine. I'm over it," I lied.

"Maybe I should just—"

"No." I put my hand on the remote to stop her from clicking it off. "It's fine. I'm okay."

They showed me rehearsing a little more, then stuck in what little footage they had of me and Tina together, bonding in a sisterly fashion. Then a grainy, distant shot appeared on-screen. I didn't recognize what it was until I saw the skateboard. . . .

"Oh!" I said. "I didn't know there was a camera. . . . Fritz had taken that afternoon off. I guess they had someone else follow me."

I immediately realized what was going on. Yes, when you looked at it a certain way, it definitely looked like Jonah and I were having a secret romantic tryst. Especially when we hugged. I hadn't realized how long that hug had lasted! It didn't help that we kept looking around furtively, as if we were checking to make sure there weren't cameras watching us— we really did look pretty guilty! I gave a snorting laugh, then turned to Tina to explain. . . .

Uh-oh.

Tina's face showed no emotion. She stared at the television screen, her eyes dead.

"That is not what it seemed like," I said.

"Uh-huh," she answered.

"Tina, you have to believe me. I can explain. Jonah showed up to ask me to get you to talk to him. He's been trying to call you, right? He was just talking to me about you."

"You didn't tell me."

That was true. And it didn't look good. But still . . . "Tina, we've barely been around each other for the past week. And I didn't know how to bring it up! I was just waiting for the right moment, and I didn't want to seem like I was interfering. . . ." I wasn't helping matters with my discombobulated explanations. I just sounded like I was making excuses. I changed tactics, and tried to explain what was going on. "Come on, this is what they do on reality television," I told her. "They twist everything and make it seem like . . . Tina!"

She got up and walked slowly out of the room.

"Come on; don't be like that," I begged, following her to her room.

"I'm not being like anything," she said. "I'm tired."

"Tina, there's nothing going on between me and . . ."

"I know," she said unconvincingly. "It doesn't matter. That's why I didn't want complications. Don't you see? Whether it happened or not, I can't afford to get upset. I've got my life in order, and it's going to stay that way."

She closed the door of her room and I heard it lock with a click.

"Tina, please," I called out, but she didn't make another sound. I knocked on her door a few times, but I didn't want to push it. My instinct was to bang on the door and scream at her to come out, but if I had learned anything about my sister, it was that the forceful, in-your-face style of Claire Marangello wasn't going to get results with her. She had gotten through her life by shutting down her feelings and moving on without thinking about them. And anyway, I didn't know what to say. I had to give her space to work it out for herself. I had to trust that she'd believe me in the end.

Besides, she had a point. I should have told her. Awkward or not, the secret was worse than the telling would have been.

I slouched to my room and melted onto my bed. Clyde padded in after me. He'd been walked by a dog-sitter, but that wasn't enough affection for the poor guy. He had no idea what was going on—just that something heavy lay in the air over his apartment. I pulled him up onto my bed with me and stroked his soft left ear while he made a snorey sighing sound and placed his paw over my other hand.

"This is supposed to be the best night of my life," I told him, and he raised a doggie eyebrow at me. "But I messed up." Blink, blink. He could have comforted me if I'd made a wee in the elevator—that, he could relate to. But screwing things up with my sister on the night of my greatest triumph? That was beyond his canine experience. All he could do was wag his little lumpy tail nub in a way that he seemed to hope would be helpful.

I turned off my light and patted Clyde's head as I stared out at the neon light that had become my night-light. I was sure to see it click off tonight. Because despite my triumph, a hollow feeling had opened in my chest, and I wasn't going to get any sleep.

Not tonight. Maybe not ever.

Chapter Eight

The next morning Tina was up and out before I even woke up. I thought I heard her walking around, and I was out of bed like a shot (it wasn't like I was having such success at sleeping, anyway), thinking I'd make coffee for both of us and see if she was still upset. But as I stumbled out of my room the front door clicked closed, and when I ran to open that, the elevator doors were already slamming shut. I ended up locking myself out, and poor Clyde almost had a heart attack when he realized we'd both left without feeding or walking him. If Fritz hadn't arrived just then, I would have been padding down to the lobby in my Hello Kitty boy-shorts-and-tank-top ensemble. No, thank you.

"Turn that thing off," I ordered him, as he stepped out of the doors and fell backward, convulsing with laughter.

"It's not on," he promised, then started laughing again. "What are you doing out here?"

"I really don't think it's funny," I scolded him as

Clyde started howling. Though it was hard to hide the fact that I was giggling too. "Come on, Fritz, open the stupid door."

"Okay, okay." He let us both in, and I made him enter first, humiliatingly aware that my butt had a giant cat-face on it. With whiskers. He patted Clyde while I hightailed it to my bedroom to get my robe, then padded out, fully covered in terry cloth and fuzzy slippers.

I plugged in the coffee pot and sat down to watch it percolate. Fritz put the camera on his shoulder, but I put a hand up.

"Just give me ten minutes," I begged.

"The other ones are on; you know that," he told me.

"I know. Just ten minutes."

He nodded, and fed Clyde while I poured us twin mugs of brown energy. On the pad next to the phone he wrote, *Just say "Ow, I have cramps" when you want me to turn it off outside.*

I read it and nodded gratefully, without being obvious about it. It all felt very *Spy Kids.* I went to my room and put on some sweats, then came out and clipped Clyde's leash on. We left the apartment, and once we were out on the street I sighed and said, "Ow. I have cramps." Fritz clicked off the camera and pretended to fuss with the film.

"Are you upset about the show last night?" he asked.

"Bingo. How did they get that footage of me talking to Jonah?" I asked.

128

"It wasn't me. They didn't tell me they were having someone else tail you. I'm really sorry."

"It's okay. I know that's how it works. The trouble is, Tina's not as experienced with reality TV as I am. I think she believes I was up to no good with Jonah."

Fritz sighed. "I should have listened to my mother and moved to Hollywood," he said.

"It's my fault. I should never have talked her into this," I said. "I just wanted to be in the show. In *Twentynothings*. I got what I wanted, but it's not really working out so great."

"Give her some time," he advised. "She'll come around."

"I hope so." Clyde finished up his little job, and Fritz turned on the camera just in time to immortalize me picking up his poop in a plastic bag from D'Agostinos. That's right, folks. Glitz, glamour, and fame: That's TV.

I felt just like the poop in the bag as I returned to the apartment and restlessly tried to get ready for the matinee show. It was seven in the morning, but I felt too weird and anxious and sad to do anything much. I decided to go over to the theater and do some rehearsing on my own.

As I sat in the quiet, deserted theater, I felt a calm settle over me. I used to look at my mom's face in church, and I was always amazed at the way, no matter what else was going on, or how loud she'd been screaming at me on the car ride over, all her cares would fall away once she sat down in the mahogany pew. Me, I never felt that way about church—maybe it was the itchy lace tights she made me wear—but here, I understood how a place could make you feel calm and centered.

I had a mini boom box with the pianist, playing the show's music, recorded onto a tape. After a long, luxurious warm-up, I hit play and ran through all my paces in the show at half-mast energy, just reminding my body what it was supposed to do at different points. Then I picked a few problem areas—the places where the choreography in my mind deteriorated from clear, bright footprints on the stage into a muddy mush of shuffles—and went over them a few times. I sat down and sang my songs quietly, the piano on the tape my only accompaniment.

As I put myself through the rigorous physical workout, mental concentration, and artistic creativity of making everything seem new no matter how many times I'd done it, I noticed that all my worries fell away. And I started to realize something new about myself. It wasn't the applause that made me feel whole. It was the work. It was making something feel complete, using the raw talent I was born with and the skills I'd picked up along the way. I probably would have felt almost as good peforming in a cave. Hell, I got a charge out of performing for an audience of my stuffed animals when I was, like, five.

This was what it was about. Not the adulation, but just getting it right, putting it together. Even the critics in my head were starting to sound like trusted friends: They weren't there to tear me down. They were there to make me do better.

As I was running through my big song, calling up memories to make the emotion more real, I suddenly realized I wasn't alone. Jeb was standing in the doorway to the theater, just watching me. My voice cracked, and the song petered out. So much for appearing cool in the face of pressure.

"You sounded good," he said. "Keep going."

"If you need the stage . . ." I offered, noting that Fritz had tracked me down, too, and was getting all this on tape. I couldn't help but notice that despite the fact that I was wise to what a dog he was, Jeb still looked as handsome, hot, and cute as ever. God, I hate my heart sometimes! Not to mention my hormones! He was wearing loose-fitting cargo pants with heavy boots, and a tight sleeveless T-shirt that . . . Never mind! I didn't even notice what he looked like. I was a total professional.

"No, no," he said, walking down the aisle toward me. "But I was thinking . . . I mean, I know you have stuff you're working on, but if you and I could run through our first song, I'd appreciate it."

"The first song." The love song, he meant. It was hard enough to sing it to him in front of an audience, letting myself feel the attraction I was trying so hard to fight.

Did I say professional? Professional. Cool as a cucumber and professional as a . . . professor. Whatever.

"Sure," I said. "Come on up. I think we're going to have to get out of here soon, or we'll be here when the audience starts filing in."

"That'd be a bonus." He laughed as he did that leaping-up-to-the-stage thing that made my heart dip into my stomach.

"Not if we suck," I pointed out, and he laughed again. He seemed a little uncomfortable. Obviously because he knew I saw through his nice-guy (hot-guy) exterior to his dangerous real self. But I did want this show to be as good as possible. So I rewound the tape to the piano accompaniment to our love song and pressed play.

I'd like to say we immediately reentered that other-worldly place where nothing matters but the work, but that's not really what happened. It was hard. It was hard singing to him, "You're the missing piece in my jigsaw puzzle; you're the way that I stay sane." And when he looked in my eyes and sang, "You're the word that calms me down; you're the music that soothes me deep inside," I could almost swear there were real feelings behind his eyes.

Of course, we're actors. We're supposed to make people believe the truths we're singing about. Besides, he was probably thinking about singing to Paula. Or to himself.

But just for a moment I felt a flash of feeling. Weird.

As we finished up both the song and our little dance number, the theater was starting to come to life. Tech guys were fiddling with the lights while the ushers began unpacking their boxes of Playbills. And the other cast members were trickling into the back-stage area.

"Who's making all that racket?" Malaika called out from near the dressing rooms. "Are you trying to make us all deaf?"

"Ha, ha," I answered with a laugh. "I thought I

might try out for the touring company of *Cats*. Do you think I have my back-alley screech right?"

"Almost," she joked back.

"Thanks," Jeb murmured, and I nodded in response while I gathered my stuff and left the stage as quickly as possible. Paula was standing in the wings, her wide blue eyes like two little angry flames, her arms crossed across her chest. It's amazing how ugly a pretty girl can get when she's glaring jealously at a guy who's doomed to cheat on her. I made a mental note of that for the future.

"Excuse me," I said as I tried to pass her, but she just turned that glare on me, and I had to squish into the curtain to get around her. "Yeek," I said. "We were just rehearsing."

"You'd better be," she hissed.

I thought of a million comebacks, but all I did was roll my eyes. This was no time to engage in a catfight.

To my relief, the show went as well at the matinee as it had the night before, so it wasn't just beginner's luck or some kind of freak onetime occurrence. The same magic came back when the curtain went up, and we all felt bonded by whatever muse was in charge of us. Well, almost all. Paula gave me a nasty hip-check just as I ran onstage for a scene, and I stumbled momentarily. But I let that slide off. Paula was no match for the great feeling I got onstage, and the audience was full of people who'd paid for their tickets. I owed them a solid performance. Paula I'd take care of later.

Or she'd take care of me. The truth was, the hip-check left me feeling a little off-kilter, and I almost had a mini meltdown. It seemed to bring up everything that had been bothering me: not just my refusing-to-die attraction to Jeb, but my worry over my relationship with Tina and even my old heartbreak over Joey. I had to force myself to imagine a little girl out in the audience, just like I'd been a few years earlier. This was her one time seeing this show, and I didn't want it ruined by my emotional upheaval. So when I saw Paula and Jeb still holding hands after we finished our bows and the curtains went down, I felt a stabbing pain in my heart. But it didn't show on my face.

"Come on, girl. You're a fantastic Tinka; that's all that matters," Malaika said, giving me a tight hug.

Okay, so it didn't show much.

Before I could hit my dressing room, Fritz showed up with a backstage assistant. He was training that camera right on both of us, so I knew there was some kind of news the reality show wanted to catch my reaction to.

"Some friends of yours are at the stage door," the stage-door guard told me. "I'm supposed to bring them back here; is that okay?"

"Who is it?" I asked.

But Fiona, Baxter, and Pete had already been shown back to my dressing room, and they appeared right behind him. I shrieked, causing both Fritz and the assistant to take a step back. Hey, I couldn't help it! These weren't just my best friends from back home in New Jersey; they were my fellow survivors from last season's reality show. We'd been through, like, a *war* together. So the fact that me, Fiona, and Pete were shrieking and climbing all over each other (I have to hand it to Fiona's boyfriend, Baxter: For a former jock he's pretty open to the weirdness that is the other three of us) was not so bizarre.

"I didn't know you guys were here!" I yelped. "Ohmigod, why didn't you tell me when you were coming?"

"Fiona thought you'd get nervous," Pete said. "She wouldn't even let me yell out your name when you came onstage. Is she a big spoilsport, or what?"

"I just didn't want more pressure on you," Fiona explained. "Anyway, the *Unscripted* producers gave us the tickets, and we had strict orders not to tell you we were coming. I guess so they'd get your surprise on camera."

"Of course, we could have gotten around them," Pete muttered, rolling his eyes.

"But it was fun to surprise you," Fiona finished his sentence. "You were great. Claire, you were so, so great."

"You were perfect! I'm so jealous," Pete added.

"You'll be here too," I told him. "Thank you so much, you guys. Believe me, it hasn't been all fun and games."

Baxter gave me a big, warm bear hug—he's quiet, but sooo sweet—and then I squeezed Pete and Fiona one more time.

"Let me get changed, and we can catch the dinner special at Ollie's," I called out.

"I can't believe I'm catching the dinner special at Ollie's," Fiona complained as my door closed in her face.

"Feel like a tourist?" I yelled to her.

"Another bridge-and-tunneler, only coming into Manhattan for the matinee." She sighed. "I guess I'm really a Jersey girl now."

"Hurry up; I'm starving," Pete complained. I went back out to meet them, introduced them to Fritz, and we left the theater, still clinging to each other and giggling.

"When do I meet Jeb?" Pete asked.

"Dude," Baxter said warningly.

"Sorry," Fiona said. "We've barely heard from you, and all the 411 we have is from what we watch on TV. And we all know how reliable that is. It looked like you were about to get together with him, and then it was over before it started."

"Well, in this case, the show got it right," I told them. "Let's just say I saw the real Jeb, and he was nothing but a fancied-up Joey. But it's okay. I'm superprofessional now, and I can hear his name without turning into a puddle. But I'm pretty sure he took off already, probably running home to have a quickie with Paula between shows. Or maybe he's got some groupies to cheat on her with. I don't care, though. None of my business."

"Well, I'm convinced," Fiona muttered.

"And I think he's a greaseball anyway," Pete added. "I just wanted to see in person how ugly and unworthy of you he is."

"I wish he really were ugly," I said as we went into Ollie's, a huge noodle shop in the middle of Times Square, and went up to the second level so the presence of Fritz wouldn't disturb (or attract) too many other diners. "It'd make things easier. Do you know that Joey's been e-mailing me? I guess the cameras add a little something, huh?"

"He tells anyone who'll listen he used to be your boyfriend," Fiona revealed. "He even has a picture of the two of you up in his locker. I think he's betting the heartbroken-guy-dumped-by-the-celeb act will get him more chicks."

"Dork," I said. "Whatever. He's a loser."

"What about your sister?" Pete asked. "What's it like, getting to know her?"

"Ohhh . . ." I got a little deflated. "I don't know how to answer you. If you'd come in yesterday, I would have told you everything's going really well. But after the show last night, she kind of got weird. . . . I haven't been able to talk to her about it."

"It's hard to understand, if you haven't been through it," Fiona pointed out. "We had no idea how things could be twisted until we saw ourselves on camera. Even when you were there, you start to doubt your own memories."

"Plus, she's just so different from what I'm used to," I said. "In my house, we scream out our feelings about everything that's going on. We're so on top of each other, there are no secrets, and we're always talking things through."

"Or trying to kill each other," Pete added. "Remember when Theresa hit me with her brush because I was between her and you? I thought she broke my collarbone."

"Yeah, there's that too," I admitted. "What about your mom, Fiona? How's she holding up?"

"Oh my God, she's so much better." Fiona started

filling me in on adventures in New Jersey, and we ordered practically everything on the menu. Before you could say "moo shoo pork," we were having such a good time throwing most of it at each other, I completely forgot I'd ever had a single problem. It is so amazing having friends like that. You know? I think that's why people go to their high school class reunions even when they're old and decrepit. Because high school is the time when all your problems hurt you the most, and the people who get you through that time, you always feel grateful to.

"Come on; I'll show you backstage," I announced. "Maybe we'll run into Jeb after all. Anyway, you guys have to meet Malaika, and if Seth's there, I'll ask him to yell at you so you can see what it's like!"

"No, thanks!" Fiona put her hands up in mock surrender. "I saw him on the show. He's a scary-pot."

"Tell me about it." I turned to Fritz. "Oh, pleeease don't tell him we said that," I said to the camera. "He'll make me run laps around the dressing rooms!"

I wasn't serious that time. We all knew how to play the reality-TV game by now: Let your fun be filmable, and everyone gets what they want. We'd developed certain rules when the show came to Hamilton High: Bypass the cameras only when it's really, truly necessary, or the producers will start to notice. Let some embarrassing stuff happen on camera, or they'll put cameras in more embarrassing places. If it kept Mary-Ellen happy to send Fritz to watch my reunion with my friends, then that was fine—she'd given me my Broadway debut, so she deserved that.

"Hey, wait," Baxter said as we walked through the

138

bar area of the restaurant on our way to the door. "Isn't that Jeb on TV?"

We all looked up at the ceiling-mounted JVC in the corner. That *Access Tinseltown* gossip show was on, and sure enough, there was the face that launched a thousand sighs.

"Hey, can you turn the sound up?" I asked the bartender. "I'm in a play with him."

You've got to love New York. Without batting an eyelash, the bartender hit his remote, and we heard the narration, read sternly by a blond, blow-dried news babe who seemed to think she was Walter Cronkite in panty hose.

"Jeb Razor, of the popular boy band 2 Hot 4 U, has been trying to make a more serious name for himself," she said. "He's taken a hiatus from the band, and just last night debuted on Broadway in the popular modern-day musical *Twentynothings*. But it seems he's taken his rock-star lifestyle with him to the Great White Way. As this exclusive footage shows, he went out after opening night, and according to a female companion, it wasn't just excitement that kept him partying till the wee hours of the night."

"What the . . ." I said. "Female companion? That could only be—"

A silhouetted figure popped up. I guess if you didn't already suspect who it was, it was a pretty good disguise. But I'd know that compact little body anywhere. Not to mention that oversize hair clip she always wears. The girl on TV could only be . . .

"Paula!" I breathed. "That little rat."

"I thought you didn't care about him," Pete said.

"Because of what he did," I told him, still mesmerized by the TV screen. "He's a dog, but he's not a druggie. If that's what she's saying . . ."

". . . I couldn't believe it," the silhouetted Paula said, her voice clear as a bell. "I mean, this is his big chance, you know? He's got a whole cast depending on him. But he was acting like . . . I was shocked. Just shocked."

"Wow, for a Broadway star, she's not a very convincing actress." Fiona snorted.

"Well, someone's convinced enough to put this on TV," I pointed out. "And you know how people love to believe everything they hear."

Nobody knew that better than us. Because of last year's show, everyone on the planet was convinced Fiona was a snotty troublemaker one week, and a saint the next. It was like whatever they saw on that little screen was the gospel truth, even when it contradicted itself. I suddenly felt a little sick for even agreeing to be on another show.

The newscaster was back. "According to this exclusive footage, it appears Jeb Razor is using some sort of drug in the VIP room of a nightclub. As you can see, something is definitely going up his nose—which means his career might end up going down the drain."

A grainy image of Jeb appeared using his allergy medicine. It looked like it had been shot using one of those digital cameras in a cell phone. Of course, Paula had a phone like that.

"Oh, my God, that little two-faced, spotlight-stealing egomaniac," I seethed.

"Jeb Razor has always flown low on the gossip radar," the announcer continued, while archive footage of Jeb with his band flashed onto the screen. "While some of his bandmates were well known for their lush lifestyles, wild parties, and banner break-ups, Jeb seemed like the nice one, which is why his fans dubbed him Charlie Brown."

"His manager planted that," I told them. "He hates it. But it's true, he's always kept himself a little distanced from the rest of the band."

The announcer's face returned to the screen. Her expression was all fake-concerned and mock-sorry-to-report-such-sad-news as she wrapped up her libelous bulletin. "Could it be that it was all just an act?" she asked. "If these reports have it right, this high-flying heartthrob may be headed for a big fall."

"God, their metaphors are unbelievably cliché," Fiona muttered.

"Guys, I have to get back to the theater!" I yelped.

"Claire, you don't have to do anything," Fiona told me, firmly. "If this guy did you wrong, you don't owe him anything."

"I know what you're saying," I told her. "Getting myself pulled into a scandal like this—it could cause me more trouble than it's worth."

"And stop your career before it even gets rolling," Pete added. "Sorry," he said to Fiona. "I couldn't resist."

"But wrong is wrong," I pointed out. "I just have to hope I learned enough last season to know how to stick up for someone without taking all the attention onto myself."

"Claire," Baxter said.

"Yeah?"

"I mean . . . are you sure he's not using drugs?"

I thought about it for a moment. Baxter was right: I had to at least consider the possibility before I went charging in there to fix everything.

"As sure as I can be," I said. "This show means everything to him. He worked harder than anyone else to get himself in shape to make it great. And he didn't even sip champagne the night we were out. He might be a male slut, but he's not a crackhead." I gave Bax a hug. "But thanks, big guy. I can always count on you to keep me thinking straight."

He patted me on the back and we headed back to the theater. We were still half a block away when I saw a bevy of camera-toting photographers and reporters gathered around the theater. As Malaika got out of a cab, they descended upon her like a pack of hungry rats attacking a day-old sandwich in a Dumpster, running over curious tourists in the process.

The paparazzi had arrived. And I was heading straight into their midst.

Chapter Nine

"Um, guys," I said, turning to my friends.

"We're here with you," Pete said, gripping my arm tightly. "We're going to rush those suckers like this is an extreme game of Red Rover. Before you know it, you'll be back in your dressing room."

"I don't know. I don't think we're getting through."

"Maybe we should create a diversion," Fiona suggested. "We'll get their attention and you can sneak in past them."

"Through the stage door," Baxter pointed out.

Fritz's cell phone made a blurpy sound as he used the walkie-talkie function on it to call one of the stagehands. "You're all clear," he said. "The paparazzi heard that you were out with your friends, so they're expecting you to come in the front with them. If they go walking past you can sneak right in, just like Baxter said."

"You're the best," I told him.

"Do I look all right?" Pete asked. "Am I ready for my close-up?"

"You look fantastic," I said. "You look like you're saving me from having to fight through those barracudas."

"I can't believe *you're* avoiding the spotlight," Fiona teased me.

"I know. It's amazing how much I've matured. Thank you so much, you guys. It was great to see you. And this is above and beyond the call of friend duty, for sure."

"Don't worry about it. We'll see you soon. In person, not on TV." Fiona gave me one more hug, linked arms with Pete, and started down the street. Baxter looked back at me dubiously, and I gave him an encouraging thumbs-up. I don't know how that guy deals with us crazy-heads, but he's like a rock. He followed behind Fiona and Pete, glaring protectively at the press people as they got closer to the front of the theater. Fritz followed them, to further throw the paparazzi off the scent. Meanwhile I saw a stagehand crack open the stage door, and I ran inside before anyone could spot me.

"Thanks," I told him. Through the metal grate I could see Fiona, Pete, and Baxter getting questioned about everything from Jeb's alleged drug use to Paula's bra size. It was nuts—they were getting jostled around, and the flashbulbs were going off so fast they looked like strobe lights. They chatted for a while, but once they saw I was inside the stage door, they abruptly headed for the subway. That's when the reporters realized I wasn't around, and they started looking all over the place, as if I'd vanished in front of their noses.

What a bunch of dopes. What a way to make a living!

I know—look who's talking: the girl who pimps herself on reality television to get an acting job, right? Well, I guess irony suits me.

It was actually pretty quiet backstage. Subdued, I guess. People were preparing for that night's performance, which was good, I supposed. It meant there would be one. Malaika's dressing room was next to mine, so I knocked on the door to see if she was there.

"Hey. Oh, they ripped your shirt," I said.

"It's all right. I think it goes with the rest of my costume," she told me, though she looked a little weary and freaked out. "Maybe I should add it in."

"It looks cool. Kind of *Flashdance*-y. So has Paula shown up yet?"

She shook her head. "I heard a rumor that she's already been contacted by a casting agent and is on a plane to L.A. But I'll bet she shows up five minutes before curtain and just hopes we don't break her legs before she can go on. I'm sure she's going to get fired."

"I hope so," I fumed. "She's such a conniving little wench."

"Yeah, but she's not the only one they are looking to replace," Malaika told me.

"What do you mean?"

She held up a finger, and I heard Jeb's big song

being rehearsed on the stage. With someone else singing it. "What the . . . ?"

"You'd better go see what's going on. I need to drink some tea or something. That was crazy out there. If I wanted to get mobbed by reporters, I would have killed somebody, not gone into theater."

I laughed. "I'll go see what I can find out. Take care of yourself."

Enid came waddling over with a steaming mug for Malaika. "They're up in the balcony," she said to me.

"Thanks." I headed up to the second level, where there was a semiprivate landing outside the box seats. Sure enough, I found Seth bawling Jeb out. And if I thought he was tough before, when he was just trying to coax a decent performance out of a semiprofessional cast . . . well, now he was apoplectic. As in, furious beyond measure, and scary as hell.

"This is a disaster!" he shouted.

"But it's a lie," Jeb yelled back.

"I don't care! I don't care if you're freebasing during intermission, I can't have this kind of mess outside my theater! The audience can't get through the crowd. The publicity is horrible. And if the critics wanted to hate you before, they're going to be savage now. Not just on you. On the whole cast. I'm not going to let you drag this entire show down, pretty-boy."

"None of this matters," Jeb told him. "I can do this part; isn't that good enough?"

"No! This is a *business!*" Seth howled. "I need people in seats to keep this play running. It's all fun and games for you, something to do between putting out platinum records and going to the MTV awards, but this is my life; it's real theater. I should never have said yes to this stupid stunt-casting. I thought it would bring a new audience to the theater, but it backfired. Big-time. I've got audience members that can't get through the crush of reporters to show their tickets to the ushers, and a tourist out front got shoved so hard, she's got a black eye—and she's threatening to sue! This has to stop now, or the whole show is going to go down the drain. I can't have you ruining it for the rest of us. You've got to get out of here."

"Dude, you can't—"

"You're fired, Jeb. I can't replace you for tonight— the actor we found to temporarily play your part just isn't ready. But after the show I want you to clear your stuff out of the dressing room. And leave through the front, so those reporters out there follow you."

Seth stormed down the stairs. "Seth . . ." Jeb called after him.

"Enjoy your performance. It's your last one!"

Believe me when I say I wanted to run out of the shadows and confront Seth. But what could I say? That I didn't mind the attention? That this was all Paula's fault? My opinion didn't matter. And Seth was right about the paparazzi attention—it was distracting, and it wasn't going to fill the theater.

Besides, he'd made that crack about "stunt-casting." As in, putting people onstage who didn't deserve to be. And I was example number two of stunt-casting that could easily backfire. He'd just turn his wrath on me, and probably can me too.

Jeb stood there, pale and shaken. I watched him clang open the door to the box seats and sink into a chair. I didn't know what I'd say or how I could help, but something drew me to him. I followed, opening the door softly and dropping into the seat beside him.

"Great seats," I said. "Do you know someone in the cast?"

He looked up at me, and a surprised smile flickered through his gloomy expression. "I used to," he answered. Then he slumped down in his seat, looking like a miserable kid who just found out his puppy's been put down.

"I'm sorry," I told him, putting a hand on his shoulder. To my surprise he put his arms around me and pulled me in for a long, warm hug. I wasn't sure what to do, so I sort of stroked his head in a way that I hoped was soothing.

"I didn't mean to eavesdrop," I murmured. "I was just trying to find out what was going on. I should have said something, but—"

"No. There's nothing you could have said," Jeb mumbled from somewhere in my cleavage, where his head was now resting. "He would just have cut you, too."

"But it's not fair. You're great in your part. You're fantastic," I told him. "You're amazing onstage. Seth was being an idiot—you're more than just a pretty-boy. You're really an actor, and you can't let this stop you from doing it again."

He shrugged, then got a sly look on his face.

"Wait a minute," he said. "So you still think I'm a pretty-boy?"

"No, I mean you're more than that—"

"But you do like the way I look."

I was flustered. "I mean, of course. But that's not really—"

"So why'd you dump me?"

I think I blushed. I felt like I was blushing. I'm really not a blusher, so I don't know for sure, but chances are, I was a shade of red that would match the stage-lights.

"I . . . uh . . . I didn't think we were really—"

"You disappeared. We were just starting something great, and I lost you before it ever got rolling. So now we're not going to be working together after all. Tell me why."

"Sheesh. For someone who was all heartbroken, you got over me pretty quickly."

He groaned and sank back down in his seat. "Don't remind me," he lamented. "I knew Paula was trouble."

I didn't say anything to that. Like "duh" or "that's an understatement" or "that'll show you what happens when you hang out with a fake-blond skank, you boy-tramp." Aren't I so restrained?

"But I was so mad at you," he continued, "and she was so . . . available. I just went out with her to get back at you."

Wait a minute. What? "Get back at *me?*" I stammered, flabbergasted. "Get back at me for *what?*"

"For using me. You know. I gave you access to my

149

trainers, and the minute you got good enough for the show, you lost interest in me."

"Oh! Oh, no way!" I sat up. "Oh, my God, I never thought of it that way. Jeb, that's not what was going on. Not at all. I can see how you'd think that. But that wasn't what I was doing!"

"Then what was it?"

I blinked at him for a moment. I was distracted by something. Something in the way he was opening up his feelings to me. In the sadness of his questions about why he lost me, where I'd gone. Then it hit me.

He was just like Jonah, knocking on the door in Tina's heart and finding it slammed shut in his face, with no explanation.

I felt like a jerk.

"Claire?" I snapped back to reality. He had a quizzical expression on his face.

"I was scared," I admitted. "My old boyfriend was a major player. He'd always make me think he loved me, and then he'd cheat, and I'd find out about it after the fact. When I saw you with all those girls at the club . . . I got scared to be with you. I knew I'd always be fighting for your attention."

Jeb gave me a sad smile. "You'd never have to fight for anything," he told me. "You've got my attention. All of it."

With that, he sat up, too, and leaned forward. I felt a wave of panic build up inside me, but I closed my eyes and told myself that the past was the past, and I had a future to think about. The wave broke over my head, as if I'd ducked under it at the beach. And the next thing I felt was Jeb's lips on mine.

I dipped my head so the angle was better, and his arms snaked around me, pulling me into his lap and enveloping me in the strongest, safest embrace I'd ever felt. My arms crept up around his shoulders as he cradled me, and I felt his tongue slip warmly over my lips to meet mine in a sexy, electric dance.

"I'm so sorry," he murmured when we came up for air. "That was the stupidest move. And it backfired. Can you forgive me?"

"If you can forgive me," I whispered back, still touching my lips to his as I spoke, feeling the tingle of contact as they pulsed with ultrasensitive feeling. "I never gave you a chance. I froze you out. I'm sorry, too."

He smiled. I saw it, and put my hands on his cheeks so I could feel it, too. "Well, you feel pretty warm now," he pointed out, and we both laughed.

"Ahem," a voice behind us coughed.

"Enid!" I yelped, and tried to get up without falling over.

"Relax," she said. "I'm not your chaperon. I'm just telling you it's almost showtime. You kids have to get ready, toot-sweet."

With a gasp I realized I was way behind schedule. No matter what else was going on, we had a show to do. And the curtain was going to rise no matter what. We had to put our boiling-over emotions on the back burner and get our butts backstage!

Chapter Ten

So you know how I described our first night, and how we were, like, one unit in the great spiritual quest of putting on a fantastic show for our audience? Well, I can't say the same for this night's performance. I'll tell you the truth; it was weird, from start to finish, and we definitely did not feel like one team.

For one thing, Paula did show up, but Enid told us later that the stage manager kept her sequestered from the rest of the cast (and from Seth) until it was time to go on. If Seth was hard on Jeb, he would have torn Paula limb from limb. Not that I wouldn't have liked to see that—but we did have a show to do, and we were barely up to speed ourselves. And Malaika had told me about the production company's money troubles: They didn't have understudies prepared to go on for us. They'd have to train new cast members in a day or two. If they were lucky, some of the old stars would come back for a few encore performances.

None of us knew exactly what was going on, even

as we took our places for the opening number. There we were, in the dim gloom of the stage before the curtain went up, and it was funny, because we were in our poses but we were shifting our eyes around like crazy, trying to see what was going on. There was a hole where the character Lenore stands, and we had no idea who'd show up to fill it. Suddenly I heard scuttling footsteps in her spot and dipped my head to check her out. Yup. It was really Paula. You could feel a ripple of tension pass through the entire rest of the cast, emanating outward from Paula. I've got to hand it to her, though. She kept it together and managed to face us, even if it was in character and only on stage. I don't know if that makes her brave or just incredibly fake. Or unbelievably committed to her character. I'll never know—she's not someone I'm going to hang out with, ever.

Anyway, so we did the show. And at first it felt cold. Our opening number was shaky, and I felt like the audience was watching curiously to see what we (the actors) would do, not caught up in the story or caring what we (the characters) were going through. That was hard. It felt a little depressing.

But despite the problems, we had created a strong bond. We were an ensemble cast, no stars, no standouts, so I think one by one we forgot about the problems we'd been having and started living the story of the show. Nobody was really comfortable being onstage with Paula, but with each other we were as real as we'd ever been, and somehow we made it work.

Anyway, Paula's character was a prissy little whiner

who annoyed us to death, so maybe that made it work better.

The other weird thing, of course, was between me and Jeb. Since the first show, the tension between us—me fighting my attraction to him, him yearning for me (now I knew!)—had given our performances a certain tension, I guess. But now! Now that we both knew how we felt about each other . . . oh, my God! When I looked into his eyes onstage, as we talked about our relationship, it was almost hard to tell when I was Tinka and when I was Claire. The same deep well that opened in my heart when we kissed in the balcony, opened again onstage for everyone in the audience to see. It was really scary to be so . . . naked. Emotionally naked. And I think the audience could tell. I think our performance was better that night than any other.

Of course, there was the bittersweet knowledge that as good as it was, it couldn't last. The performance, anyway. Because if Seth was serious, he was going to toss Jeb, this amazing performer, out of the show, just because of some bad publicity. It was enough to make me lose faith in the whole theater business.

Well, sort of. Maybe not. Being onstage and inhabiting this character still felt too good. Wow! Jeb and I were on fire.

And then . . . oh, man! When we had to break up? When we had to scream at each other and then sing our hearts out? I think we surprised ourselves. Because we really did feel angry toward each other. I was pissed that he'd wasted time on someone like

Paula. And he probably had leftover fury about me using him, even though I didn't. Plus, there was the fact that I'd wasted so much time running from him. He must've been mad about that, too. Whatever— we channeled it into that heartbreaking scene, and it was so real to me, I almost got sick. I'm serious, I had to fight to calm myself down.

Of course, having to fight to calm myself down is nothing new for Miss Hissy Fit. But this time I was focusing that feeling into a role, and it worked. My hissy fit had a place to go. I'm telling you, harness it right and this acting stuff is really like therapy.

Like I said, the audience could sense something was going on. Despite the paparazzi, the tabloid shows, the gossip, despite everything, the cast came together and made the audience care about the people living in this illegal downtown squat, fighting a hardscrabble, scrappy battle to keep the home they'd taken over. The characters weren't perfect, but they had a story to tell, and we told it, and the audience listened. It was amazing!

When we held hands for that final curtain call— they called us out for, like, three of them—there was such an electric current between us. Jeb was next to me, holding my hand, leaving Paula all the way at the other end—I won't deny how good that felt. And when the curtain came down for the last time, he didn't let go. Everyone else clapped and hugged, just because it had been such a wildly emotional performance by all of us. But Jeb and I locked lips again, expressing the passion of our characters and of ourselves.

But that couldn't last forever. Enid interrupted us with a phlegmy cough.

"Seth wants to see you," she said to Jeb.

He started to walk away, but I still had a hold on his hand, and I followed along.

"You should stay down here," he said. "I don't want you getting caught up in this."

"I already am," I told him. "I'm caught up in it because I'm caught up with you."

"I can't let you do that. This show means too much to you."

"So do you." I held his hand firmly. "I know I can make it as an actress. If it's not here, then it'll be somewhere else. I'm not going to let you go again."

He shook his head, but he didn't shake his hand loose. Not that he could have. I think at that point the skin of our hands had fused together. Wherever he was going, I was going.

At the moment, we were going to talk to Seth. Yikes, was it too late to reconsider?

Actually, Seth was strangely quiet. He was sitting in his office with his head in his hands, surrounded by piles of paper and general clutter.

"The show was fantastic," he admitted without looking up at Jeb. "I shouldn't have said you couldn't do it. You're fine in the part."

"Thank you," Jeb said quietly. We were both waiting for the inevitable "but," and sure enough, it was the next word out of Seth's mouth.

"But even if I wanted to, I couldn't keep you in the cast," he added. "I got calls from our biggest investors. They're running scared. They hate the publicity."

"What if you tell them I'm leaving too?" I asked. "If you lose two cast members—three if Paula leaves too—the show will have worse problems than bad publicity."

Seth still couldn't quite meet our gaze. "Well, it's sort of a moot point," he muttered.

"How's that?"

"They didn't like the whole reality-show thing in the first place," he said. "They only went with it because they needed to fill more seats—they thought they'd get good publicity. When they couldn't control everything, they panicked." He finally looked up, and his eyes were like two black pools. "I'm afraid you're out, too."

I felt a tiny explosion in my heart. Of course I knew he might take me up on my offer to quit the show, but I was kind of hoping he wouldn't. Hearing him say my run was over . . . it stung, I won't lie. But right after the sting came a flood of relief. If my time on Broadway had to end, at least the tension and problems that came with it would end, too.

"That's crazy," Jeb said. "You can't fire her too. Because of me? Because of what someone said about me, that's not even true? Don't we get due process?"

"In a court of law, yes. But not on Broadway." Seth shrugged.

"You shouldn't do this to me. And you can't do this to Claire."

"It's out of my hands. Some of the old actors are coming back, and we're training your replacements starting tonight."

"Come on," I said, tugging Jeb's arm. "Jeb, come on. Let's just get out of here and think things over."

Seth's head was back in his hands, and I, for one, was too tired and numb to get into an argument about right and wrong. It was midnight, we'd done two shows, and we'd had all kinds of emotional meltdowns. It had been the longest Saturday in the history of Saturdays.

I guess Jeb agreed with me, because he quietly turned away from Seth and walked out the office door. We stopped off in our dressing rooms to change and get our stuff. The theater was nearly empty—Paula was long gone—and pervaded by an eerie silence, punctuated only by a few clangs as the stagehands did some repairs on the minimalist scaffolding that made up our set. We walked up the aisle, turned back at the same time to look at the stage, and then left the theater for what I figured would be the last time ever.

We stood outside for a moment.

"I feel . . ." I shook my head. "I don't know how I feel."

"Relieved," Jeb said.

"Exhausted," I added.

"Pissed?"

"Pissed. And resigned."

Jeb put his arms around me. "And happy."

I cuddled into the cave of his arms and chest. "Actually, mostly happy," I murmured, a little surprised. He kissed the top of my head.

Without saying where we were going, we just strolled into Times Square. It was actually pretty empty. I mean, not Hamilton, New Jersey, empty. Our town square actually turned off its traffic lights after midnight. But empty for Times Square. Just a few cabs circling around, a car here and there, the ever-present Fritz trailing behind us like the vapor steam behind a comet. And steam rising mysteriously from the manhole covers. It was like a movie set, but with a chill of late summer that gave me goose bumps, reminding me that this was my life.

"What a wild ride," I said. "A few months ago I was just a high school kid in New Jersey. Now I'm a Broadway veteran with a celebrity boyfriend."

"I'm a boyfriend!" Jeb laughed.

"Oh! Is that okay?" I gasped. "I just assumed—"

"Of course!" He pulled me in for yet another kiss, which you might be getting tired of, but I certainly wasn't. "God, that's what I've wanted since I saw you."

"But what about all that stuff I was worried about?" I asked. "All the girls. All the pressure. Everything we do is going to be scrutinized. And all those girls—"

"Hey, I've been doing this for what, five years?" Jeb pointed out. "The first couple years . . . I won't lie, they were crazy. And then I had to figure out who I was inside all the hype. Why do you think I came here, to do this? I'm trying to keep it real." He shook his head. "I can't promise you everything's going to be perfect. Fame can be a real pain. But it also has a few perks. And if you'll just trust me a little and be patient, I promise you I'll try my best to keep my head on straight."

160

I was still peering up at him, and I guess I looked a little dubious.

"And the girls," he said. "I'll tell you the truth—after the first couple months, I got really turned off to the whole groupie scene. You can ask my bandmates. They really thought there was something wrong with me."

I wanted to believe him. Oh, what the heck.

"Well, I don't," I said. "I think you're just fine."

I wrapped my arms around his middle and rested my chin on his chest, looking straight up into his eyes, and he planted a tender kiss on the tip of my nose. I know New York is the city that never sleeps, but that night, somehow, Times Square was just me, Jeb, the moon, and good old Fritz.

New York *Daily Post*
Gossip Scene
Blind items: Guess what hot, modern Broadway hit has suddenly turned turkey? This reporter hears that the show's producers and investors got spooked by a high-profile scandal involving one of the show's stars and canned half the cast in a blind panic, citing concern for the impressionable young teens they'd been hoping to attract.

But tongues are wagging as it turns out the impulsive decision is backfiring big-time. In the few days since the gutting of the cast, lackluster performances by quickie understudies, plus a tired rendition of her earlier role by formerly-brilliant Lenore Evelyn Boquart (did anyone tell the producers that it's a bad idea to have a five-month-pregnant ingénue?) have left audiences rushing out to the box office in droves, spending their intermissions demanding their money back as the show's shiny-headed director slowly sinks into a deep depression. The show, in this case, must not go on.

Meanwhile, a certain former starlet, who spilled the beans on her handsome costar and former love interest, has taken off for the Left Coast to try to consider a bevy of offers from various C-list sources. We hear she's going to show up in *Playboy*, though not even as a centerfold. Oh, well, that's life in the big city, kids.

I lay in my bed gazing out at the bright blue sky, wiggling my toes to wake myself up. My alarm clock told me it was past nine-thirty in the morning. This was the latest I'd slept since this wild ride began, and I was definitely enjoying the feeling of being lazy. Soon enough I'd have to pack up and go back to Jersey, but *Unscripted* was letting us stay here through the end of the month. Fritz was still filming me, but there wasn't much to see now that I was out of the show. Just a lot of me and Jeb tooling around the city.

Yum. Jeb. I ran my tongue around the inside of my lips, which were actually getting kind of sore from all the kissing we'd been doing. He'd taken me out to Brooklyn to show me his old stomping grounds. It was awesome, especially the busted-up charm of old Coney Island, a sweet little amusement park all the way at the other end of the borough. They have this roller coaster—the Cyclone—that's made of wood, so not only is it terrifying to go on, it also makes a ridiculous racket. Fun stuff, I'm telling you. It had been a great couple of days.

Of course, the truth was, as wonderful as it was to be with Jeb and see the city and have time to myself, none of this was as special or as fulfilling as being in the show. Yes, it was nice that the blisters on my feet no longer bled all over my white socks, and that my muscles had a chance to bounce back. But I missed . . . not the pain, but the work. As beautiful as the sunny beach of Coney was, I preferred to spend my days in a dim studio with a rattling fan and ten sweaty castmates.

I wiggled my toes a little slower. There was one more problem, and I was starting to realize that it was bigger than a Broadway show. Tina and I still hadn't been able to talk things through, and it seemed like our big meeting and life-long friendship was a bust. She'd been logging mad hours at work, probably to avoid me. After a while, I just stopped trying to ambush her in the shower or after work. Then I called her at work a bunch of times, but I just got her voice mail. I felt just like Jonah: leaving messages that never got answered by the busiest lawyer in the world. And as for Jonah—ugh, I felt so horrible, I didn't even want to try calling him. I hadn't heard his voice on the answering machine—he probably thought it was best just to finally give up. His last, desperate shot at getting Tina back had missed by a mile and ended up backfiring, big-time. And it was all because of the stupid show I was on, and the fact that I'd tried to use it to forge a relationship with my sister—or the other way around. My stupid chase for fame had screwed up everyone's lives.

I stopped wiggling my toes. My relationship with Jeb was the only thing going right. And as wonderful as it was, it wasn't enough. I was going to have to face reality soon. My dream was down the drain, my sister hated me, and . . . oh, that blue sky was too damn cheerful. I pulled the sheet over my head and rolled over.

Bang!

I sat up. My bedroom door had been slammed open by Tina, looking extremely official in her best black suit. Her hair was clipped back in a severe bun, and her feet were in a brand-new pair of sky-high pumps. Fritz was right next to her, his camera trained on me.

"What the . . . ?" I stammered.

"Come on, get out of bed," Tina commanded with a strength and authority I frankly didn't know she had. "Fritz, leave her alone to get dressed. I want you in something official-looking. That means not from Bebe or Arden B., you got that?" Tina waved a finger at me, and I nodded in response. I was too shocked to speak. I don't know what was more surprising— Tina's new attitude, or the fact that she was in the same room with Fritz and wasn't hiding from him.

"Hurry up!" she told me. "We're due at the lawyer's office in one hour!"

I gave Fritz a baffled look, but all he did was shrug. Either he didn't know, or he wasn't telling. From the way Tina was bossing him around, he was probably terrified. The door slammed.

"Tina?" I called out. "What lawyer? Does this mean you're not mad at me?"

"Not now," she called back. "Just get ready. I'm turning on the shower so the water will be hot."

"But—" My feet got tangled in my sheets as I tried to leap out of bed, and I almost took a header. "Wait, what lawyer?"

The door opened a crack, and Tina popped her head in.

"Not now!" she snapped. "Shower! Clothes! Chop-chop!" She hung one of her lawyer suits on the inside of my doorknob and disappeared again.

Today's lesson learned: Never try to argue with a lawyer!

Chapter Eleven

There's something about the end of summer. You know? One day it's scorching-hot August, the streets smell like garbage, the air is thick with humidity, and it feels like you'll be wearing flip-flops forever. Then you notice the nights are getting a little chilly, the daylight doesn't last as long, and the next thing you realize, you're buying back-to-school clothes and eye-balling the Halloween display at Stop & Shop. Don't you just think it's the most melancholy feeling?

All right, all right, just kidding. I'll tell you what happened next, but I'm going to set it up for the most dramatic effect. After all, I may be growing up, but Claire Marangello will *always* be a drama queen.

So here's the scene: Tina, Jeb, Clyde, and I were sitting on the big white couch in the apartment, watching *Unscripted*. Fritz was in his usual post, across the room, sitting on a stool with his camera hovering in front of him. When Tina came on the screen, you would have thought we were watching the final quarter of a Knicks game from the way we screamed. Even Clyde barked, though whether that was from pure fright or because he saw his mommy on TV I'm not sure.

I mean, Tina was on fire. She was in the conference room at the office of the producers of *Twenty-nothings* and she was like Al Pacino in *And Justice For All*. My quiet, shy, straitlaced sister was yelling, throwing her arms around, and gesticulating like . . . well, like *me*.

Meanwhile, the actual me—the me that was also on TV with Tina—just sat there, wearing Tina's suit, with my hands folded and my eyes wide.

"You look like you have no idea what's going on." Jeb laughed.

"I didn't! I was totally clueless. This crazy woman yanked me out of bed, and the next thing I knew, I was Exhibits A, B, and C," I told him.

The board of directors was obviously terrified. I couldn't quite keep up with the ins and outs of what she was going on and on about, but it involved a lot of phrases like "classic case of employer discrimination," "the rights of my clients to have private lives," "due process," and "totally specious allegations that violate my clients' privacy and could have been disproven, if their private activities were any business of yours, with a simple blood test." The gist of it was obvious: She wanted them to hire Jeb and me back, pronto, or she was going to open up a can of whup-ass so vicious, they'd be afraid to produce anything more than a morning poop.

At least, that's how it looked to me. She was as intimidating on the screen as she'd been in that conference room. Maybe even more so. The fact was, Tina had an amazing TV presence. She was *very* photogenic. The camera absolutely loved her.

Now, the fact was, the show was in trouble without us, and the producers knew it. Tina knew it, too, but she had a couple years of experience going up against business types, and knew they'd have a hard time admitting they made a mistake. So it was up to her to drive the point home.

"This is the tape that the informant released to *Access Tinseltown*," she announced, wielding her remote control as if it were a weapon. The VCR in the corner of the conference room flickered on, and the familiar grainy footage came up: Jeb seemingly hiding in a recessed corner of the club, his hand over his face, making odd sniffing motions. It didn't look good. For a moment the people on the board of directors smirked at each other, like, "Yeah, we knew we were right."

"I hate this part," I told Jeb.

"I could have gone the rest of my life without seeing that again," he complained.

"But what you haven't seen is this," Tina-on-TV added. "I have additional footage from that same moment, taken at a different angle. A much closer angle. Please observe."

She flicked the VCR on again, and we all saw Jeb in the same outfit, the same night, doing the same thing—only this time, he was visible from the left side. And it was clear what was up his nose: the green cap of a Flonase bottle. Now the rest of the world saw what I already knew: The poor guy was just suffering from allergies, not partying like it was 1985.

We all let out a whoop and threw popcorn at the TV. Clyde started barking again.

"Oh, shush, Clyde, come here," I called, because there was more.

Jeb's handsome face filled the screen, and I couldn't help but cheer again.

"Gosh, but you're dreamy," I told him.

"Maybe I'll autograph your training bra." He smirked.

"Training bra? Why I oughta—"

"Come on, listen," Tina insisted.

"Tina was right," Jeb said to the camera. "What I do in my private life should have no bearing on whether I can stay in a show. Yeah, I know I'm a role model, but I'm also human, and I think if I had a problem and went to rehab, my fans could handle it. The important thing was that my performances were consistently good. But for the record . . ." He held up an official-looking white sheet of paper. "Bam," he said. "Clean as a Boy Scout."

"And now for the pièce de résistance," I said. Jeb and I returned to the theater, walking through the front doors like we'd done so many times. Seth met us just inside the doors. "Good to have you both back," he said. "Do you think you'll be ready for the next performance?"

"Definitely," TV-Jeb told him.

"No doubt," TV-me added.

"Yaay!" I cheered. "Okay, let's watch *Friends*."

"Wait," Tina told me.

"When did you get so . . ." My voice trailed off as I saw what was on the screen. "Ohmigod. Oh—my *God!* What?"

Jeb scrunched down between two cushions and pulled a throw pillow over his face.

"Please help me," he groaned.

There we were, me and Jeb, in the balcony of the theater on the day we were fired. I knew we kissed a lot that day, but . . . Yikes! We looked like Siamese twins joined at the mouth! It was like a nature documentary on the mating habits of actors!

"Turn it off, turn it off!" I shrieked. This was mortifying!

"Fritz, you're a jerk," Jeb complained, and I suddenly realized he was right. I sat up.

"Fritz! How could you?" I accused him.

It was so infuriating that I couldn't see his face—as usual, his eyes were covered by his camera. But I saw his mouth curl up into a cat-that-ate-the-canary grin.

"Oh, don't you dare get mad at him," Tina ordered, intercepting the pillow I tried to chuck at him. "He's the one who took a night off to trail Jeb and Paula and get that close-up of the Flonase bottle. So if he wanted to have a little fun with you two, too bad."

"Aaaagh!" I threw myself across the couch in mock-agony. "Fine. You know, you've gotten really bossy since you had this little adventure with the producers." I paused and thought about it. "Thank you, Fritz," I said grudgingly. "Why were you following him, anyway?"

"Something smelled bad," he shrugged. "I had a feeling Paula was up to no good, and I wanted to keep an eye on Elvis here." He shook his head. "I really need to get a life."

"He came to me with both tapes," Tina said, shooting him a grateful smile as she pulled her legs up under her in that way that makes her look like a little kitten. "Before he even took it to the producers, he let me know what was going on so I could build my case. And I let them know I had it, so they couldn't suppress it—that Mary-Ellen Murray wanted to do that, because she liked the drama of you two getting fired. Little did she know just how much drama I could give them. And it was just what I needed to really nail these guys."

"Which you definitely did," I said. "Have I thanked you enough times yet?"

She laughed and shook her head. "Really, it was fun," she told me. "And the partners in my law firm loved it. My boss tinkled in his torts when I showed him the tabloid-TV report, and the new footage I had that could disprove what Jeb was getting accused of. He ate it up, and he loves the publicity the firm is getting from all this. They haven't made me partner yet, but it looks like I scored major points. And I did get a fat raise. Of course, that's only if I log more hours in the courtroom, in front of a jury. . . ."

". . . Uh-oh!" I squealed.

"No, I have to tell you—the only reason I blasted through all that research and stormed in on the board of directors that way was because I was so angry and wanted to help you, but once I got rolling, I realized it was no big deal. It was like getting thrown in the ocean and suddenly realizing I could swim."

"Like a champ," Jeb said. "You're really good!"

"Thanks." She blushed. "But it's all because of Claire. She gave me the boost I needed, and showed me how it was done."

"I'm just glad you did it," I said, giving her a mighty squeeze around the shoulders.

"Besides," she went on, "it was the least I could do after acting like such a weirdo for the past week."

"Don't, don't say it!" I said. "It's okay! I was just afraid you were mad at me. . . ."

"I know! I was just having some kind of emotional . . ."

"Meltdown? Hissy fit? Tantrum? I guess we really are sisters," I pointed out. "Maybe I taught you more than you realized!"

"I just wasn't used to letting my feelings get the best of me. I'd always been in such tight control. I'd been paying my mom's bills since I was twelve, for God's sake. So to realize I actually cared what Jonah did . . ." She shook her head. "I knew you weren't doing anything with him. What upset me was that the possibility would even bother me."

"What were you, a robot?" Jeb wanted to know. I whacked him in the leg, but she just smiled.

"I was trying to be." She shrugged. "I've lost a lot in my life."

We all got quiet then. The TV blared, on to the next show after mine, but none of us knew what to say.

"Like my dad," I finally blurted out.

173

I couldn't quite see Tina's face. It was tilted down toward her hands, which were sitting, pale and folded, in her lap, looking like two white shells against the bright pattern of her cotton skirt.

"It's still strange to think about," she admitted. "That you had this traditional family life while I was such a nomad. That the little man I met at Sardi's was the giant bogeyman who I'd blamed for all my problems. I can't even picture my mother and him together."

"A different place and time," I said.

"I guess . . . I mean, I'm a grown-up now, and I'm not going to live my life under the shadow of something that happened when I was still in diapers. But getting to know you hasn't been as easy as I thought. I've had to come to terms with the fact that my dad really does exist out there, and that his life went on without me. I've had to face the fact that you had a lot of things that I didn't have, but I have a lot that you didn't have, too. And . . . oh, it's just so weird having a stranger be your family. This whole experience has forced me to let go of Tightlaced Tina and become something . . . messier." She looked at me, her gray eyes searching for the right words. "It's been fantastic, but so much harder than just being on my own and in control of everything in my life. There don't seem to be any easy answers."

"Life isn't a TV show," I said, sitting up and putting my hand on hers. I flicked a look at Fritz, whose little red light was like an eye trained on us. "With all due respect, real life doesn't wrap itself up in a neat little bow at the end of its hour-long slot. It takes time to

174

work stuff out. I'm just glad I know I have a sister. It doesn't have to be a perfect relationship."

I saw Tina's eyes well up with tears, and she flicked them away with an embarrassed chuckle.

"Oh, this is a very special episode of *Unscripted*," she joked.

"Sure, maybe we'll have a guest appearance by Heather Locklear," I said, and we both laughed a little.

"What about Jonah?" I finally asked. "I mean, you said it bothered you when you realized you really cared about him. So does that mean you're finally going to call him?"

"Please." Tina snorted. "He finally gave up. I'm sure I succeeded in totally, completely scaring him away. Who needs a workaholic girlfriend who can't choose between emotional freak-outs and freeze-outs?"

"So you're just going to let it go?"

"I think the decision's been made for me. He hasn't called in the past week. I guess I have to work through whatever I have to work through, and start over with a clean slate."

"I dunno," Jeb offered. "I don't think life works like that."

Tina shrugged. "Well, it's gonna have to this time."

The door buzzer let out its signature obnoxious shriek, making all of us jump out of our seats.

"Thank goodness, I was starting to wonder what I was doing here," Jeb announced, as he bolted off the couch to press the buzzer and ask Carlton what was up.

"Your Chinese food is on the way up," he told us.

"Well, it's about time," I complained. "We ordered before the show even started."

"If they forget the cold noodles in sesame sauce, I swear I'm going to . . ."

"Drag them into court? My God, I've created a monster!" I joked.

Jeb went to open the door, and Tina got up to get the plates. I saw her go to the kitchen and grab her wallet, and then freeze, staring toward the door.

"What's the matter?" I asked, stepping toward the . . . hallway to see for myself. "Don't tell me he forgot the . . ."

Fritz was on his feet, his instincts telling him this was, indeed, a very special episode of *Unscripted*. I had to hurry to stay one step ahead of him as I got up and peered down the hall to see . . .

Jonah, holding the Chinese food bags and gazing at Tina.

They stared at each other for about a hundred years (or maybe five seconds, but they felt like a hundred years, as the rest of us had no idea what to say or do), and then she rushed over to him and threw her arms around his neck. Jeb deftly took the bags out of his hands and carried them over to the counter, grinning widely the whole time.

"I'm so sorry," Tina wailed, her voice muffled because her face was crushed into Jonah's neck. Her feet left the floor as he picked her up and hugged her back, so hard I thought I'd have to rescue her. "I really love you, I truly do, I don't know what got into me. I'm so sorry I didn't call you back. I'm sorry!"

"I know, I know," Jonah murmured back, not even caring that Fritz's camera was trained upon him in this moment of total and complete romantic surrender. But I did.

"Come on, Fritz," I said, grabbing a couple of platefuls of noodles and rice and shooing him back into the living room. "Nothing more to see here."

"Oh, come on, I'm supposed to . . ."

"Here you go, buddy," Jeb said, grabbing him around the waist and lifting him bodily off the floor.

"Wow, you're strong," I complimented him as they toddled into the living room. I followed behind, carrying the food, leaving Tina and Jonah to work things out in the foyer, the kitchen, or the bedroom, whichever suited their fancy.

"I hate you guys," Fritz groused. "These two being apart was the missing piece in the *Unscripted* puzzle. If they're getting back together, it really does wrap things up. The audience would love to see this . . ."

"Fritz, I hate to say it, but some things are just more important than sweeps week and a neat, tied-up ending."

"But this one was real," he complained.

"And that's the beauty of it. It's real, so it doesn't need to be on TV," I said, as I settled back into the couch with Jeb and flicked the TV back on. Fritz sighed and resigned himself to filming nothing but chopsticks and white takeout containers.

"I guess they've got their next episode," Jeb commented as he mixed up the cold sesame noodles.

"And then it's just three more, till the show ends and I go back to school," I said.

"Unless they extend our contracts. Then, who knows?" Jeb said.

I thought about it. Who knows . . . about anything? I could end up back at Hamilton High for my senior year, or I could get tutored while continuing on Broadway after *Unscripted* ended. Or something else could happen . . . another show, a TV audition, a recording contract . . . Or it could all come crashing down. But one thing I knew for sure: Whatever happened, I had a family that was a little bigger, a circle of friends that included one truly dependable boyfriend, and more inner strength than I had ever realized. And I had at least another month to hang with Jeb, get to know my sister more, and apprentice myself to the only craft I've ever wanted. So no matter what the future would bring, I felt like it would be okay.

I curled my legs under me, Tina-style, and turned the TV up so none of us could eavesdrop on Tina and Jonah's murmured conversation. They sounded happy enough. Meanwhile, my muscles were already feeling stiff and unresponsive from their few days off. I was going to have a hell of a time getting back into show-shape in the next day or so. I'd have to be at the theater at the crack of dawn to get in extra rehearsal time—my blisters were bound to open up again, no matter what I did—ugh, and that pancake makeup was going to make me break out. Yeah, after this last night of laziness, I was going to have to really work my butt off to keep myself in top form for the show. . . .

And I couldn't have been happier.

Turn the page for a special sneak
preview of **KATIE MAXWELL**'s

What's
French
For
"EW!"?

Coming in May!

Subject: Guess what? I'm going to have a baby!
From: Em-the-enforcer@englandrocks.com
To: Dru@seattlegrrl.com
Date: 4 April 2004 9:19pm

Did you freak? Heh heh heh.

Hola, chica, we're back from our trip to London! Oh, wait, I'm supposed to be getting ready for Paris. Bonjour, chicklette. Nous returnez-vous from Londonez. Or something like that. You know, if I wasn't getting to spend two whole glorious parent-free weeks in Paris—city of loooooooooove—I would just give up trying this whole French thing, because it's majorly diffy! The grammar and stuff you have to learn! Sheesh! Like I have time?

Anyhoodles, when I got back from London, Holly called and said she heard from Chloe T (you remember her—she's from Pennsylvania and has braces) that we're getting our babies this week. Chloe T's dad works for the company that makes the software they use in the babies, so she should know.

"Very cool and about time," I told Holly, putting some Wanton Woman Red polish on my toenails. "I hope I get a girl. Because, you know, dealing with a baby widdle-stick is just going to be too embarrassing. OHMIGOD! I just had a horrible thought! What if the baby is like a real one? What if it can pee on you? My friend Dru's cousin had a baby boy, and we were playing with it, and when Sara went to change it, it peed all over the front of her!"

"According to the pamphlet Miss Naylor gave us, they don't really pee, they just kind of excrete the water they suck in from the baby bottle," Holly said. "Chloe T says the reason they were delayed getting the babies to us is because they were upgrading the software, so now we'll have LuvMyBaby v4.75, which has the advanced behavior card, and a bigger memory chip so the babies can be used for up to a month without having to be taken in to have the care data downloaded."

"Ew. Who'd want a baby for a month? A couple of days is just fine with me. Short enough to be fun, and then it's bye-bye to pretend motherhood and hello to us in Paris having oodles of fun with Devon."

"I don't think I'd mind having one for a month if it was a nice baby," Holly said, sounding thoughtful. She's been doing a lot of that lately. It's kind of worrying me, to tell the truth. It's like she's become that woman in the opera your mom made us see last year—you know, the one where the woman had TB and was coughing up blood and guts and stuff, and was dying a lonely, tragic death. Camille, that's the name of it. Holly has been Camille-ing lately. "I think it sounds like a very interesting experiment, although Mum says if she'd had a LuvMyBaby when she was going to school, she never would have married Dad and had us. Whatever sex baby I get, I just hope I don't get a colicky one. Chloe T said some of the babies are programmed to be fussy. I can't deal with a fussy baby, not when I'm going to go to Scotland for the weekend. You know how I break out if I don't get lots of sleep, and what will Ruaraidh think if I show up all spotty with big black bags under my eyes?"

"I'm telling you, apricot scrub is your best friend." I eyed my Wanton Women Red toes and decided another coat was needed. You know my toenail polish motto: two coats is good but four is better. "Brother told me he read up on the *Show Teens the Horror of Becoming a Parent* program, and found out that the LuvMyBaby people set the babies to be really cranky so you never, ever want to have sex. I think that's cheating. I mean, some babies have to be good, don't you think? Mom says I hardly ever cried. 'Course, she thought I was mental or something because I didn't talk for a long time, but still, I was a good baby. So I don't buy all this stuff they're feeding us about the babies being ultra realistic and stuff if they're just really safe-sex propaganda."

"What do you think I should wear when I go to Scotland?" Holly asked, totally ignoring what I was saying, only in a nice way. I didn't really mind, because she wasn't sounding Camille-ish when she talked Scotland, even though she is getting to leave school early to go. I have to stay through the last of the semester because I missed that week last month when I had the flu so bad that I puked my guts up every time I got out of bed. Life is so unfair.

"Em? Are you still there?"

"I'm here, just thinking." I sighed, but quietly, so she couldn't hear (am I like the most considerate person in the whole wide world or what?).

"Oh, good. So what do you think—the gypsy and lace outfit, or not?"

"Not. You want to look sophisticated and elegant for Ruaraidh, not like a reject from a really bad seventies rerun. Go with the pink mini mod, that's the look that says what you want to say."

"I'm not exactly sure *what* I want to say," Holly waffled. She's been doing a lot of that lately, too. "But I suppose the pink mini does make me look older."

I know you were wondering how things are going between her and Ruaraidh of the eleven fingers, but there's not really much to tell. They haven't seen each other except for the one weekend at the beginning of March when Ruaraidh came down to meet her mom and step-dad. Holly said her mom kicked up a bit of a fuss 'cause she was dating a guy who was eighteen (she didn't seem to mind that he had an extra finger on his left hand, though), but Holly'll be sixteen in a couple of months so it's not really that big an age difference. I mean, Devon turned nineteen in February, and you don't see Brother or Mom saying anything about me dating him. Then again, I will be seventeen in just two weeks (woohoo! Can't wait!), and I *am* very mature for my age and all.

Anyhoo, Holly and I talked about what she was going to wear when she went up to see Ruaraidh, and what she would say, and what he was likely to say back to her, and how she should respond to that, and what he would think of the latest sweater she'd knitted him (She's up to five now. I'm still trying to knit my darling Devon a lump-free scarf, but I've only got a couple of inches that actually look like scarf.), what she was going to do when he kissed her, and all that other stuff you have to talk about when you've been away from your BF for months and months and months. You know how she is—obsessed! It's hard to get a word in when she's going on and on and on about Ruaraidh, but I'm sure that's just because she misses him so much.

Aren't you glad I'm not like that?

Not that I could be, since Dev has been soooo attentive (*fans self*). Because he's perfect, and because I'm a GF extraordinaire, I called him after Holly went over what she should say to Ruaraidh for the fifth time. Five is my limit—indulging in conversation practice more than that makes you sound stilted, like you've been . . . well, practicing.

"Snuggle bunny!" I said when Devon answered his cell phone (they call them mobile phones here, which I guess makes sense, because what exactly *is* a cellular?). "I'm back, and guess what? I'm going to have a baby!"

Devon made an odd sort of choking noise. "You're . . . you're what? But we haven't . . . you told me you wanted to wait . . . you're still a...is it Fang? Is that it? You told *me* no, but you've been shagging my best mate?"

Whoa! I wanted to tease him, but suddenly Devon sounded all pissed off and hurty and stuff. "Of course I haven't . . . *you know* . . . with Fang. He's my best friend, too." [Besides, you, of course. You're my BFF, but Fang's a sweetie and he's my best guy friend. Next to Devon, but Dev doesn't count because he's a BF, and BFs rank higher than just a guy friend. Where was I? Oh, yeah. Devon.] "I would never do that to you, Devon, you know that! I'm the one who told you that you couldn't date any other girls if we were going to go together, so why do you think I'd tell you that and not do the same?"

"But . . . you said you're pregnant—"

I made a face at the phone. I know it was a teensy bit mean, but I was a little insulted by what he said. You know that my main concern with him all along has been that he's the flirtiest guy on two legs, and I wasn't absopositively sure he could just be with me without going for another girl, but he has, which is why he's the perfect Mr. Emily. "I never said that, you great big silly pants. I said I was going to have a baby. And I am. From Wednesday to Friday, then I have to turn it back in to Horseface Naylor."

Devon said something I'm not going to repeat because I know you don't like potty mouth words, then heaved a big sigh. "Oh, the pregnancy prevention doll. I forgot they are doing that at Gobotty now. They didn't when I was there."

"It's going to be fun. Brother is already threatening to

go away if I leave my baby lying around so it annoys him. And just think, while I have the baby, you'll be a daddy!"

Devon swore (I'm going to have to punish him for it, oh yes I am!). "It's only for a few days, I don't suppose I'll have much to do with it."

"Sure you will! I have to help you on Wednesday pick out what to wear to Paris, and then on Thursday you promised to take me to the new Johnny Depp movie, so we'll have lots of quality baby time together. I have to turn it in on Friday afternoon before I fly to Paris. Everyone else is turning theirs in on Saturday, but because I'm leaving early, Mom asked the school if I can get rid of it on Friday. Horseface was not happy, but ha ha ha ha," I said as I twirled around my room. "I'm going to be spending two weeks in the most romantic city in the world with the most romantic, nummy, totally snogworthy guy in the whole world, and she has to stay home and download baby data."

"One week," Devon said carefully.

"What?" I asked, stopping the twirling (it was making me a bit barfy—you know how easily I get dizzy). "What?"

"I promised Dad I'd go fishing with him, so I'll only have one week to spend in Paris with you, Emily."

My heart, a previously happy, GF to a fabulous BF heart, a madly in love heart, a heart filled to the rim with thoughts of all the wonderful ways I was going to kiss Devon in Paris, dried up into a shriveled little thing that looked like your great-grandma Mabel's ears before she died. And you know how icky one-hundred-and-eight-year-old ears can look. "Noooooo!"

"I'm really sorry, love, but things haven't been too good between Dad and me since Mum kicked him out. I know you'll be busy with the intensive French classes and outings, and won't miss me at all that first week."

"Of course I'll miss you," I said, thinking about going into full pout mode. I decided not to only because a pout doesn't translate well on the phone. "The whole reason I was looking forward to Paris is because you'll be staying in a really nice hotel, and I can stay with you if I want, and we won't have the Parental Units breathing down our backs every second and coming up with feeble excuses to interrupt us while they make sure we're not having sex. Besides," I said, taking a really deep breath, my tummy going all woobidy at the thought of what I was going to say, "my birthday is on the eighteenth, and I was going to let you give me a special birthday present."

"Another one?" Devon asked. "I already bought all of the items on the list you gave me."

I gnawed lip. I know it's bad to gnaw when you're trying to have happy, plump, kissy lips, but sometimes a girl just has to give in and gnaw, and this was one of those times. "This is something special. Something you'll like, too."

"Not another Motörhead CD?" Devon asked suspiciously.

"No. *Special*," I said, wondering if I had to spell it out to him. "Really special. Something you've never had before. Well, you've had it, probably, although I don't know for sure, but I'm almost positive you have, not that I care if you have, because that was before you gave me my ring, but I haven't, and that's what's special."

There was a silence on the other end of the phone for a couple of seconds, then Devon asked, "Another *Buffy* DVD?"

"No!" I rolled my eyes. I mean, sheesh! He was a guy!

He was supposed to know what I was talking about without me having to say it, right? "S-P-E-C-I-A-L. Picture the scene—you and me, alone in your hotel room on my birthday. At night. Just the two of us—"

"Are you talking about a romantic dinner?" Devon asked.

"—just the two of us," I said, kind of grinding the words between my teeth. How on earth was Devon taking all those hard engineering classes if he couldn't figure out something simple like this? Obviously I was going to have to give him a bigger hint. "The two of us . . . with no clothes on."

Five more seconds of silence. "You want to play strip poker?"

"SEX!" I yelled into the phone. "We're going to have sex!"

"We are?" Devon asked, then he worked the shock out of his voice, and quickly said, "Oh. I didn't realize you'd changed your mind. Erm . . . are you sure, Emily? You were awfully adamant when you made no sex one of the terms of our dating."

"That was because we hadn't been boyfriend and girlfriend before, and I didn't want you calling me names like Aidan did when he thought I was going to but I didn't."

"Emmy, love," he said in that wonderful breathy voice that made me go all girly. "You know I'd never do anything like that to you. I agreed to your terms because I'm mad about you just the way you are. You're smart and sexy and funny, and you put other people's feelings ahead of your own."

I stopped kissing my pillow with the iron-on of Devon's face that I had printed from his picture. "That last bit was too much, buster."

"Was it?" He sighed, then did a little laugh. "I wondered if it was, but I figured it was worth a shot."

"I might not be Saint Emily, but I suppose if you really, really, really have to go with your dad so you can stand around killing innocent fish for a week, I won't be too heartbroken. I'll only cry for three days straight. And I'll write really bad poetry about my heart breaking. But that's OK. I'll survive. *Somehow.*"

"That was about as subtle as *my* attempt," he laughed, and despite the fact that I was really disappointed by the fact that we wouldn't have two weeks together in Paris, I felt pretty happy. I had told him The News, and he sounded happy about it, not that I thought he wouldn't be, because he sometimes got, you know, *that way* when we were kissing, so I know he wants to and all.

We talked for a bit more about what we were going to do in Paris (he's going to take me to a really hot nightclub!), then Brother barged into my room and asked me if I'd like him to set up an IV line so I could ingest my meals intravenously in order to talk continuously on the phone without ever taking a break and giving someone else a chance to receive a phone call. Fathers! I'm telling you, if he weren't paying for me to go to Paris and have sex with Devon—I mean, to attend an intensive French class—I'd tell him a thing or two.

Gotta go, my toenails are done and I want to give Devon his good-night call. He's so nummy! I'm so happy! Life just can't possibly get any better than it is now, except after The Night, of course. Everything will be better after that!

Hugs and kissies,

~Em

Subject: Re: OMG! OH MY GOD!
From: Em-the-enforcer@englandrocks.com
To: Dru@seattlegrrl.com
Date: 5 April 2004 7:58pm

Dru wrote:
> You're going to do it? IT??? With Devon? OHMIGOD!
> You have to tell me everything! What are you going to
> wear? What are you going to do? No, wait, I know
> what you're going to do, I mean, how are you going to
> act? OMG! This is so major! I haven't even *thought* of
> doing it with Timothy, and here you are making a sex
> date! OMG, OMG, OMG!

Sheesh, Dru, you don't have to go all Springer on me! It's not that big of a deal.

Well, OK, it is, it's the biggest thing that ever happened to me, and that includes the night Devon gave me my ring, which up to this has been the biggest thing, but don't you think that *doing it* qualifies as the biggest thing? I do. Getting into Harvard would be close, but I really do think this is bigger.

OK, I just had a spazz attack thinking about just how this will be the most important moment ever, the moment when I know Devon loves me more than anything else, the moment when I'm sure that we're absolutely perfect for each other and that we'll spend the rest of our lives together, so in order to remain sane, we have to stop talking about it. 'Cause otherwise I'm really going to freak out, and you know that's never pretty.

What if I don't do it right? What if I'm, like, bad? What if Devon hates it with me and is too nice to tell me? What if I don't like it? What if he looks at me and doesn't get *that way?* What he if thinks I'm too ugly to do it with? OMIGOD, I'll die! I'll drop down dead right there in his hotel room, ugly, naked, and still a virgin, and Mom and Brother will have to come to France, and they'll KNOW! They'll know I was too ugly and horrible at it for Devon to do it with me, and if I wasn't already dead, I'd die again, and they'll probably put it on my headstone.

Here lies Emily, so ugly, no one would do it with her.

Aaaaaaaaaaack!

All right. No more sex talk. None. Zippo. Zilch. Nada. *Rien!* (that means nothing in French).

So, for a non-sex topic, let me tell you about . . . um . . . my baby. OK, there's a bit of sex there, but only pretend sex, not real sex, not the kind of real sex where if the love of your life, a guy so nummy you want to drool whenever you see him, decides you're just too horrible to do it with, you'll die. Not that kind of sex.

We had our first day of Baby Boot Camp today at school. Horseface Naylor (yes, she still hates me, although I don't know why, I'm a perfect Saint Emily in her class. Well, except for the time I made whinnying noises when she walked into the library. And the time she found that cartoon of her that Holly and I had been drawing. And the day I slipped up and called her Miss Neighsmore. But other than that, I've been perfect) . . . what was I saying? Oh, the baby stuff. Horsie is taking over the week of baby training.

"Becoming a parent is not a decision you should take lightly," she said, glaring at me. I couldn't tell if she was glaring at me just on general principle, or if she knew I was planning on doing *it* with Devon in a couple of weeks. "Creating a child is an action that will have an effect on you for the remainder of your life. In order to bring home just how important it is that you consider the ramifications of engaging in sexual contact, Gobottle School has gone to the enormous expense of purchasing the very latest in realistic baby simulators, which you will all receive tomorrow afternoon before you leave school."

I waggled my eyebrows at Holly. That always makes her laugh.

"The LuvMyBaby units are programmed to wake up randomly day and night, alerting you to its needs by crying. The computer inside the unit monitors how you care for the baby. One third of this class's grade will consist of how well you care for the baby over a seventy-two hour period."

I raised my hand. "How loud is the baby? My father said he's going to stay with a friend if he has to listen to a pretend baby cry all night long."

"The LuvMyBaby creators have included actual recorded cries of babies in each unit." Her lips twisted into a grim smile. "It is a very realistic, very effective cry. I would suggest you purchase a pair of ear plugs for your father."

"Not to mention one for me," I said to Holly.

Horseface whirled around and pinned me back with a glare that would have killed a lesser girl. "If you handle the unit too roughly, or if you do not support its neck, your actions will be recorded. If you do not change the doll when it needs changing, the computer will note your lack of actions. If you do not feed the baby at the appropriate intervals, it will be so recorded on the computer chip. If you neglect, abuse, or mistreat the unit in any way, the computer will know, and ultimately," her grim smile turned particularly evil, "*I* will know. Your grade will suffer accordingly."

"There goes the ear plug plan," I sighed.

"Can we hire a babysitter?" Snickerer Ann asked. Yes, she and Snickerer Bee are still snickerers, and they're still snotty to me. I just ignore them. They're *so* juvie.

"No. Once you assume responsibility for your baby, you can't leave it with anyone else. Each of you will receive a tamper-proof wristband with a plastic key attached that you insert before feeding and tending to the baby. The key signals the computer that care is being given, thus only the assigned parent may quiet the baby."

"No babysitter?" I whispered to Holly. "Is she serious? Devon is going to take me to a movie on Thursday! I figured I'd get my mom to take care of the baby for me, but I can't do that if it's going to ruin my grade."

"Maybe it won't be that bad," Holly whispered back to me. "If you just missed a couple of hours, that wouldn't do much harm, would it?"

I waved my hand in the air again. Miss Neigh-Neigh rolled her eyes and ignored me until I added a little snap to the wave. "What is it, Williams?"

"So, how important is this baby care stuff?"

She made a kind of growl that I thought was really uncalled for. I mean, are teachers supposed to growl at students? That's got to be against some sort of law. "I have been telling you these last ten minutes just how important it is. One third of your grade hinges on your success with the babies, and those of you who are facing a lackluster grade thus far in the semester," she narrowed her eyes at me just like she was making a point or something, "will find the only way to pass is to have a nearly perfect response rate with the babies."

"But what if someone had a really important date and she had to leave the baby with her mom, and the baby cried during that time, and the parent wasn't there with her key to turn the baby off? How bad would that be grade-wise?" I figured it wouldn't hurt to ask.

"Failure," Horseface said, snapping the word like it was something brittle and she was . . . um . . . something snappy. A turtle, yeah, that's it. She said it just like she was one of those snapping turtles. "Such a blatant act of child negligence would result in a failing grade."

"Oy," I said, trying to think of how I was going to explain to Devon that our baby would have to come with us to the movie.

"Any further questions, Williams?"

"I don't suppose I can request to have a non-fussy baby?" I asked, thinking that if it was quiet, maybe I could stuff it into my big canvas book bag so no one would know I had it with me.

Horsewoman's lips peeled back in another smile. It really was a gruesome sight. "I assure you, Williams, I will do everything within my power to see to it you have the doll you deserve."

That sounded an awful lot like a threat, don't you think? I bet you she gives me an über-cranky baby just because she hates me. Which just means I'm going to be the best mom there ever was, because I refuse to let her screw up my chances of getting into Harvard just because I had the Demon Seed baby.

The rest of the class was spent creating a budget for what it costs to raise a kid. You wouldn't believe how much money it costs just to go to the hospital to have one! I'm going to have to marry someone really rich, which, luckily, Devon is. Not that I love him for his money, you understand. I love him 'cause he's all nummy and stuff. I just can't wait until my birthday when we get to do all sorts of wicked things to each other, assuming of course that he wants to do them to me . . . rats! I'm doing it again!

No sex talk, no sex talk, no sex talk.

Tomorrow we get to see the dolls and learn basic baby care, then the keys are bound to our wrists and it's Hello Mommy for the next three days. Wish me luck. With Horseface at the controls, I'm willing to bet I get the evilest of all the babies.

> So! You'll never guess what happened. Sukey and I
> were coming out of biology, and I ran right into Andy
> Forrest (you remember him, he used to be all chunky,
> and was on the chess team), and he said hi, and I said,
> like, hi (only really cool), and Sukey did the nose-snorty
> thing she does. And later, when we were at Dairy
> Queen for lunch, she told me that she heard that Andy
> had gotten some girl pregnant. Andy Forrest! Some girl!
> Pregnant! OMG!

Boy, you just don't know about people, do you? Andy sat next to me in third grade, and he didn't seem at all like the kind of guy who would go around *breeding*. Oh, hey, what happened when you told Mr. Barnes that you wanted to do your work experience at the modeling agency rather than Nordstrom's? Did he OK it? That is so cool that you talked the agency into letting you do your two weeks WE with them. Just think of all those modelly type people floating around. And photographers! I just bet you one of the photographers sees you and wants to make you an instant model!

Gotta go and finish this baby budget. We have to plan for eighteen years! Man, if I have the three kids I'm planning on having, I'm going to be broke unless I marry rich.

Something to think about, huh?

Hugsies,

~Em

They Wear WHAT Under Their Kilts?

by Katie Maxwell

Subject: Emily's Glossary for People Who Haven't Been to Scotland
From: Mrs.Legolas@kiltnet.com
To: Dru@seattlegrrl.com

Faffing about: running around doing nothing. In other words, spending a month supposedly doing work experience on a Scottish sheep farm, but really spending days on Kilt Watch at the nearest castle.

Schottie: Scottish Hottie, also known as Ruaraidh.

Mad schnoogles: the British way of saying big smoochy kisses. Will admit it sounds v. smart to say it that way.

Bunch of yobbos: a group of mindless idiots. In Scotland, can also mean sheep.

Stooshie: uproar, as in, "If Holly thinks she can take Ruaraidh from me without causing a stooshie, she's out of her mind!"

Sheep dip: not an appetizer.

Didn't want this book to end?

There's more waiting at **www.smoochya.com**:

Win FREE books and makeup!
Read excerpts from other books!
Chat with the authors!
Horoscopes!
Quizzes!

 smooch Bringing you the books on everyone's lips!